LOVE IS TRIUMPH

Old Everett King had made up his mind that both his grandsons, Sanford and Walter, would slave for the family company, as he had done himself and as he had forced their dead father to do. But Walter rebelled, fled, and hid out all winter in a Cree village seventy miles north of Quebec. Everett eventually found him, but Walter had met and fallen in love with beautiful Josephine Carbeau, which made him resist the ruthless old man all the more.

AMBER DANA

◆

LOVE IS
TRIUMPH

Complete and Unabridged

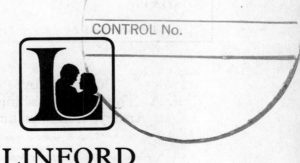

LINFORD
Leicester

First published in Great Britain in 1970 by
Robert Hale and Company
London

First Linford Edition
published 1999
by arrangement with
Robert Hale Limited
London

British Library CIP Data

Dana, Amber, *1916* –
 Love is triumph.—Large print ed.—
 Linford romance library
 1. Love stories
 2. Large type books
 I. Title
 813.5′4 [F]

 ISBN 0–7089–5545–2

Published by
F. A. Thorpe (Publishing) Ltd.
Anstey, Leicestershire

Set by Words & Graphics Ltd.
Anstey, Leicestershire
Printed and bound in Great Britain by
T. J. International Ltd., Padstow, Cornwall

This book is printed on acid-free paper

1

What is a Cree?

Cree towns were different in two ways. One, paint was rare, vertical planks formed all external walls, and below the rusted nailheads there was usually black stain. The older the cottage, the more pale and bleached became the sidings, the darker were the stains.

Paint was expensive. It also took time to apply. But more than anything else in the northern winters of upper Canada, near the fir, pine and balsam forests of Quebec Province, temperatures that hovered well below zero for weeks at a time flaked the paint off when summer came.

The second difference was that Cree towns never seemed to grow. White-men towns grew. Quebec, once charmingly provincial with its wonderful old stone parapets, was now a great ugly sprawl. Almost all the towns of Canada were like that. Except Cree towns. They were the same year after year, generation after generation. It had little to do with the fact that the young people usually left as soon as they could, although undoubtedly that was pertinent. Nor was it, as some learned sociologists said, because the Cree Indians had a declining birthrate. Just as many Crees were being born as whites, or Assiniboins, or anyone else, and just as few were dying because the same enlightenments prevailed in Cree villages as did elsewhere in Canada.

Cree villages were as constant as the land. That was the secret. If traplines failed it meant the animals were either being thinned out or were moving on. Crees then moved where the trapping was better.

If the forests were logged over, the pay for labourers, as well as the demand for them, diminished, Cree families filled their old cars and trucks and followed the other loggers.

In the old days it had been the hunting that had determined things. Now, people only hunted for sport, and it was economics that determined things. In a way it was the same. Two or three hundred years earlier a gun or an arrow or a snare brought warm furs for clothing. Now the people wore wool, not furs, and job-hunting and money brought warm clothing.

The way old Peter Sancroix who owned and operated the Partage Valley Emporium at the village of McLean put it, made sense. 'The only thing that has changed for the Cree in five hundred years, is that those accursed American redskins called Sioux got pushed out of Canada and ended up down in Montana. They were nothing but red savages. The Crees had a written language before we whites came, and they had no trouble changing a parka for a mackinaw. They were civilized people — except that those damned Sioux butchered a lot of them, making the numbers less — otherwise they would have bigger villages. But for a Cree to adapt was the simplest thing in the world. He already knew how a man has to live with nature, didn't he? Well then, what else did he have to learn, except that instead of making a parka of pelts, he had now to work in the lumber mills for money to buy his coat? It was that simple.'

John Carbeau, son of Johnny Caribou a Cree leader one generation back, grinned over Sancroix's statement, hitched a little closer to the great iron stove in Sancroix's store and said, 'You know, something I learned a long time ago when the priests were up here working round the clock to convert the Cree and save their souls from hell's-fire . . . Any kind of a convert is a hundred times worse than a man who is born into something. Pete's wife, Sarah, is a Cree woman. His children, all married now and gone, were more Cree than French, like Pete. Well, Pete is not a Cree, but he has lived in McLean most of his life, and he considers himself a Cree. So — if you want to strike a spark, say something about dirty Injuns, or lazy Crees, or maybe hint that we aren't as hard workers or can't learn as fast as whites or others and Pete will jump down your throat and try to kick out your insides.' John kept grinning. 'That's what I mean. You see? Well, when those priests made their new Catholics, they made that kind of convert. I can tell you it is a fact because my wife, who is now dead, became a convert. She made my life miserable. There is nothing worse on this earth than some kind of a convert. You take Caroline Laughlin; she smoked and drank. Now she makes life miserable for her friends who smoke or have a drink.'

It was all true. The Crees were a tall, light-skinned, dark-eyed and dark-haired people, mostly very handsome. They had been warriors, of course, but because of necessity, never because they loved war. They farmed in Canada's

5

brief and spectacular summers, other-wise they trapped and traded. Like their more southerly kinsmen, the oldtime Iriquois people, they were poets and songsters, philosophers and explorers. It was the darker-hued Indians, the fierce and lawless Sioux, who had been a thorn in the Cree flesh exactly as Sancroix had said, and the Crees remembered. Sancroix of course didn't remember; he was a French-Canadian, not an Indian. But he had heard the old stories so often as a young man he too was bitter about the Sioux, and that was what amused some of the Crees.

Nothing worse than a convert, John Carbeau had said, and how sadly true that was.

The village of McLean, in breath-takingly huge and beautiful Portage Valley, had been named for a man noted in Cree legends because he wore a skirt instead of trousers, and gaiters up his calves, and a splendid red tunic, and swung a sword like a madman when there was war. But it was that plaid skirt that made the most lasting impression. In wintertime eastern Canada not even women wore skirts. It was an incredible thing, so the Cree named their village after him.

The valley, with McLean upon the southerly rim where a forest had once stood dark, almost impenetrably deep and brooding, ran for a hundred miles northward to the first thrust of the purplish, balsam-spiked mountainsides, and to the east and west it spread much further. So distant in fact that when one of the late spring high-fogs came, and the skies closed in, down low, it seemed that there were no east-west barriers at all. However, on a sunshiny day, because the air was as clear as glass, it was possible to see the other mountains; higher to the west, and darker, than were the grey, rounder and less forbidding easterly mountains.

Portage Valley had muskeg swamps, patches of wild blueberries that ran for miles along ice-water creeks with trout in them as shiny and plump as round stones. There were also foxes and wolves, bears — in season — and edible animals as large and nearly as fleet as horses.

Of course there were the fur-bearers too, and they were again on the increase. Fur prices were chronically depressed; nowadays people bought synthetic wool and cultured furs. Nobody wanted prime pelts, or if they wanted them, refused to pay a fair price, so the animals were making a slow recovery. John Carbeau could show a visitor ten beaver-dams in a two day hike; something no one had seen in so short a walk in a hundred years.

Portage Valley was good to the people who lived in it, a few in isolated cabins near the creeks, or set in the permanently shadowed forests, but who mostly lived at McLean. But the change had come just barely in time. One or two more generations of trapping, and thinning the herds of meat animals, and McLean would probably have died like so many of the other villages had done.

Moreover, while television reception was fair in summertime, it was the magazines and catalogues people studied through the fierce, bitterly cold winters that made the young people restless. Each spring a few more went down to Quebec. When the young men returned driving good cars, wearing watches, ties, laced-shoes, they weren't Crees. And the girls, always taller, more statuesque than French-Canadiennes, looked more American than even Canadian. But then, as Sancroix had noted, adaptability for a Cree had always been very easy. It still was.

Integration? There wasn't even such a word. Crees were fair-skinned. Their features were fine, intelligent. A Cree could pass for anyone, if he chose to, but none ever bothered. And anyway, as Sarah Sancroix had once said, probably spitefully, inter-marriage had been going on for so many hundreds of years now there probably wasn't a pureblood Cree Indian left in all

9

Canada. Old Pete would just wink and grin about that. He knew for a fact it wasn't quite true, but then Pete Sancroix did not like arguments. Not even — or perhaps not *especially* — with his wife.

He and John Carbeau, though, talked about it, with a bitter spring wind rattling the old barn-like general store, lashing the windows with a sleety spray, and it was agreed that while the term 'pureblood' left considerable leeway, providing one did not seek to go back further than perhaps two or three generations, each of them could name at least a dozen 'pureblood' Cree.

'The McLaughlins,' John averred, 'are all Cree.'

Sancroix thought a moment before nodding agreement, and neither he nor John Carbeau saw anything unique in an Indian named McLaughlin.

'And there is Etienne Delacroix,' exclaimed Pete. 'But without a wife or children, and at his age, it won't matter much longer, will it?'

'No. There are quite a few of them out in the woods,' mused John. 'Not as many as when I was a kid, but still, you can stumble across their corn patches and their cabins every summer.'

Pete's dark eyes studied John. 'How about you?'

'Yes . . . Well, I think so. But I have an old gold pocket watch my father used to carry. Inside it there is some writing.'

'What kind of writing? French?'

'American. It says 'Take the best of both worlds, son.' '

Pete kept studying John Carbeau while thinking that over, then his gaze faltered and fell. He shrugged. 'What does it matter anyway, John?'

'No, it doesn't, Pete. A man is just a man. But it helps that we look alike, you and me and everyone else.'

And that of course was the wisest thing John Carbeau had said all day.

In fact it might have been the wisest thing he had said all year, even though John was a wise and tolerant and thoughtful man; a widower ten years now, with just one child, a daughter who worked for an international manufacturing company down at Quebec, but whom he only saw for a week or two, during her vacation, each summer.

Otherwise, he lived alone in his comfortable cabin just off the main thoroughfare of McLean, spent most of each winter day hovering by the stove at the store, and in summertime watched television, or smoked his pipe on the porch, or sometimes went away into the forest to visit old friends. Rarely — because Pete Sancroix could not always get away when he wished to — John and Pete went to fish the distant creeks, in summertime.

It was a good life. Crees, not even self-appointed ones like Pete Sancroix, ever had ulcers. They didn't even have a word for it.

2

A Missing Man

The blueberries ripened only in mid and late summer, but when it happened the women swarmed out across the valley with their buckets, and their children, to make the harvest. Blueberry jelly had no equal in all Canada.

There was one slight inconvenience. Bears loved blueberries too, and at that time of year, when the ravenous hunger was upon them because they had to build up their layers of fat for the winter sleep, sometimes there were confrontations.

Crees did not have any great respect for bears the way those dark-skinned lawless Sioux had. In fact it wasn't uncommon for a dozen Cree women, trailed by excited dogs and stone-hurling youngsters, to grab up cudgels and take after blueberry-eating bears.

But summer was still a little while off. Spring had come, everything was soggy and muddy and windy, which kept people from moving much, the same as forty-inch drifts of snow had limited movement. But there was a blessed difference; the thermometers were climbing steadily. It rarely got below freezing at night, while during the daytime it quite often got up as high as fifty degrees above zero, which was enough to make people dressed in warm wool pant like dogs.

Except that springtime put buds on the trees and warmed the earth so new life might stir, and brought back the small birds, and brought forth the wily and man-hating wolverine — the *carcajou* of superstitious people — and made the other alterations that meant another life-cycle was progressing, it was not a very delightful time. At least when there was perma-frost and snow, the footing, treacherous in places, was solid. In the springtime there was just mud.

But as Pierre Trudeau who carried the mail said that day he got stuck four times on the road to McLean, 'It always comes, and I suppose if we survive the winters we can also survive the thaws, no?'

But springtime in Quebec Province, at least in the uplands reaches of it where the great St. Lawrence River could not affect things very much, never lasted very long. Or perhaps it was more accurate to say that if it did linger, how was anyone to know when it became summer, for nothing changed except that the ground dried out, the roads firmed up, and trout-minnows simply grew large enough to cast soft shadows. But otherwise there was only a very gradual and subtle increase in the heat of the sun, the length of the days, the size and clarity of the huge primeval moon.

Still, because people are people, everyone had either an event or a date to point to as specifically signalling the arrival of summer. For

Sarah Sancroix it was when Pete shed his last pair of woollen underwear. For Pete it was the first day John Carbeau failed to appear at the store to sit by the crackling stove, and for John it was when he could finally walk out five or six miles into the valley and catch sight of the gaunt and scruffy old she-wolves with their dark-haired whelps leaving the low places and heading for the upland meadows where the elk and caribou and deer herds went to feed only in summertime.

Down in Quebec springtime was a red numeral on calendars and summer was a short notation under a black numeral that simply said: 'First day of summer.'

In big cities the arrival of summer, like the arrival of the morning mail, was less an event than a date; in summertime salesmen could get out to the villages, or fishermen could start readying nets, but neither could do either until an authority somewhere noted that such-and-such a date would be the time to do it.

John Carbeau did not return to Sancroix's store for a full week of seven days. Even Pierre Trudeau, who had brought a letter for John, showed a little anxiety.

'Listen, Pete,' he admonished Sancroix, 'he's not as young as he once was. He could have slipped on a rock and maybe broke a leg or something.'

Caroline Laughlin — a cousin of the old Cree named *Mc*Laughlin who lived in the woods — snorted and said, 'If John Carbeau hurt himself he would build a fire of wet wood you could see all the way down to Quebec.'

Pierre, stung by the woman's callousness, said, 'All right then — and suppose he lay out there and died? How would you like *that*!'

Caroline said nothing. Neither did any of the other people in the store, so Pierre was vindicated, and when he went over by the stove for a cup of scalding tea — his daily reward even in summertime when hot tea made him sweat like a moose — Pete Sancroix went over with him looking preoccupied.

'Every summer John goes off, Pierre. There are those old friends living out the winters in the forests. Those old Crees. You know; he goes and makes a round or two to make certain they are all right.'

'Well, and suppose he found a family that *isn't* all right, Pete, what then?'

'He'd be back, that's all.'

Pierre poured water from the copper kettle on the stove, added a pinch of ground tea from the bottle nearby, and began to stir. Maybe, as some said, instant tea wasn't as good as leaf tea, but it certainly was simpler to make.

'No telephones in those cabins,' said Trudeau. 'No doctor. Pete, there isn't enough trade in McLean to make you love it that much. Why don't you go down closer to Quebec, or maybe over nearer to Montreal, and start up a store where there is more trade?'

Sancroix's dark eyes lifted. 'All right,'

he said, in a slightly flat and hostile tone of voice, 'then tell me why you keep hauling one skinny canvas bag of mail up here to McLean year in and year out, when your seniority certainly entitles you to an easier route down by Quebec — or nearer Montreal.'

Trudeau's round face cracked a little. His tan eyes twinkled. 'Okay,' he said. 'We're even. But I still worry about John.'

'I'll go first thing in the morning, Pierre. Lord knows no one could track him in this mud, but I think I know where most of those damned cabins are.'

'Be careful yourself, Pete.'

'What? What are you talking about — be careful?' Sancroix curled his broad, low brow into a series of ridges. 'Oh, no; don't tell me you believe in the *carcajou?*'

Trudeau flushed, gulped down his tea and scowled.

'Don't be a smart-aleck in your old age, damn it. I was thinking how easy it is to slip and break a leg or twist an ankle on slimy stones. Or maybe step in someone's lost old trap from last winter. There are a dozen things that can happen to a man alone out in the valley, and you know that as well as I do.'

It was true. After Pierre had taken his limp, soiled canvas mail pouch and had climbed into his General Motors four-wheel-drive truck for the trip back to Quebec, Sarah waited until the customers were gone, then she came across to the counter where Pete was tallying the day's receipts, leaned down and said, 'I want you to take some of those truck flares and a pistol, Pete.'

He gave his wife the same flinty look he'd given Pierre Trudeau. 'What in the hell would I do with a pistol — shoot a Sioux, maybe?'

'Make a noise, what else. If anything happens you know how a gunshot makes a noise everyone can hear for miles.'

'Ahhh. I see. And if I am lying with

20

a broken back I can shoot the flares off at night, eh?'

'That isn't very funny,' said Sarah, who was actually a little taller than her husband but after so many years never stood erect near him. Still leaning on the counter she watched him finish the tally and put the slip of paper in the cash register. 'You know Pierre might be right, too, don't you?'

'That's ridiculous,' snorted Pete. 'John is snug in someone's cabin smoking kinnikinnick by a big fire every night and eating fat moose steaks.' He paused to return his wife's steady, black-eyed look. He smiled and reached to pat one of her hands. 'Look; how many summers has John done this? All right; all right, he usually doesn't stay out a full week. Well, he travels slower now, that's all. Anyway, why should he hurry home? His wife has been dead a long time — twelve years now?'

'Ten.'

'And except for one lousy week each

summer when she comes home to let her hair down and maybe do a little cooking, what does Josephine do for her father?'

'She writes him a letter at least every week, and our children — especially Angelique in California with her big house and swimming pool — do they write us a letter every week?'

Pete shook his head gently. 'But you see — I have you. John has an empty, cold house. In his boots I wouldn't want to hurry home either.'

Sarah softened, although she was not a soft woman, usually. 'Just take the flares and the pistol, will you do that?'

'Sure,' said Pete. 'It's about time to close up. Go on home. I'll close the stove off and lock up. Pretty soon with the damned tourists arriving we won't be able to close early, eh? Well, Pierre doesn't know it all. Maybe we don't make much in wintertime, but if he only knew how we made out in tourist-season, eh?'

Sarah went as far as the door, then turned to watch her husband. She was a handsome woman. As a girl she'd taken Sancroix's breath away the first time he'd seen her. Three children hadn't added a pound, and something like twenty-five years hadn't brought many lines, and not one grey hair.

He felt her eyes on him and looked up. It was still like electricity when they saw each other like that from a distance of fixty or sixty feet.

But Pete had changed. His curly black hair had iron in it and his thick, powerful torso had settled and loosened and filled. But there remained fire enough, and to spare. He said something in Cree and Sarah's arched brows dropped a notch.

'You are coarse,' she said, twisting the door-knob.

'I can't help that. I don't know the better words but I'll tell you one thing — the feeling is exactly the same.'

She smiled. 'Bring the pistol and the flares. Don't forget them. Then you can leave first thing in the morning, and I'll come down and open the store.'

After she had gone Pete rolled up his eyes. Why was it that a woman always had to repeat things over and over again as though a grown man were a small child?

Of course he would remember the damned pistol and the ridiculous flares. And he would spend several days falling into icy bog-holes and being frightened half out of his wits by screaming animals at night just outside his campfire, and meanwhile he and John Carbeau would pass by one another, so that when Pete finally returned, hungry and miserable, there would be John sitting by the damned stove smoking his pipe.

People were bad enough, but especially *women*, were the most exasperating, annoying, irritating, sometimes even infuriating things the Good Lord had seen fit to set upon their hind legs.

As for John Carbeau — when Pete found him he was going to give John a piece of his mind for stirring up all this senseless anxiety.

3

The Third Night — and Morning

Portage Valley had never flooded within the memory of man, but nonetheless it was a great bowl with the valley floor its bottom, and all spring, summer and autumn snow-water from the surrounding mountains poured down granite slopes into the valley.

In many places creeks ran brimful with icy run-off, but as any geologist could have explained, most of the run-off sank into subterranean gravel beds and was carried off in this fashion.

The Crees knew every bog, every creek, every yard of soft-sucking mud and sand and gravel. If there was much real danger someone would either have built a stone cairn to warn others, or else local tradition and talk would have passed along the warning.

In either case, since Sancroix's general store was headquarters for the villagers, summer or winter, Pete surely would have known every bog-hole. This knowledge was reassuring to Sarah, who always worried when her man went out into the valley. He was a merchant, not a trapper.

But there was another geographical aspect too. As spring gave way to summer, which was to say that as the huge snow-caps diminished to their yearly minimum, those underground gravel beds carried less water, the above-ground soil dried considerably, and the danger of something like quicksand dwindled in proportion to the rising summertime heat. In other words, as Pete toiled back and forth out in the valley, he could always find a drink of water, but it was becoming increasingly difficult for him to accidentally kill himself, which was a nice state of affairs because Pete Sancroix was not much of a woodsman, regardless of the light he viewed himself in.

The final advantage was that Pete knew just about every cabin in the forests or out upon some stony ledge in the valley itself. He and John Carbeau had been making fishing, and even occasionally hunting, expeditions out into the valley for many years. As a matter of fact they had paid for the privilege of sleeping beside some old Cree's stone fireplace with fish and meat, fruits of their explorations, in places where now only rubble showed that some old man had ever existed at all.

But the cabins were distant from one another, which was understandable since that was the main reason those people lived in the woods to begin with — to be away from other people, naturally — but it didn't make Pete's labours any easier. And also, as he profanely said aloud several times that first day of skirting the muskegs and avoiding slippery creek-side stones, not having the faintest idea which place

John was visiting made it impossible not to visit a dozen places where he was *not*, before finding the place where he *was*.

And invariably when the storekeeper from McLean showed up on someone's promontory, or came striding out of the forest-fringe into someone's vegetable patch, it caused some astonishment, not to mention curiosity.

But no one had seen John Carbeau.

The first and second days it went like that. The second afternoon it got unseasonably warm, and by evening when Pete Sancroix was mid-way between two cabins as angry as a rutting moose because he knew what was going to happen, it rained after sunset.

He had a poncho and he had a fire, but sleeping in a sitting posture was impossible and lying in muddy rivulets, even with the poncho covering most of him, was equally uncomfortable.

The following morning when sunlight came with a breathtakingly beautiful

29

dawn, water dripped from every tree and soaked him from the knees down when he pushed through brush patches. He did not appreciate that dawn. Later, though, when the heat dried things somewhat, he felt better. But by four in the afternoon he was so sleepy he decided to gather wood early and make his camp while still two miles from Jacques McLaughlin's place, then be up and on his way before daylight so he could have breakfast with McLaughlin, who was a tall, lank, gaunt, old solitary Cree widower.

There was one interruption. About midnight when his fire died to coals some half-starved wolves found him, and it wouldn't have made any difference if he'd been a seasoned Cree trapper or hunter, at the first screaming wail all the hair along the nape of his neck stood straight up. Wolves did — but only rarely any more — attack men. That wasn't what filled him with fear. He couldn't actually have defined that fear but it was both real and consuming.

Instinct, forgotten and totally sublimated in a place like Quebec, or even McLean, rose up blindly in men when they were alone in the wilderness. It was the fear handed down from perhaps ten thousand years; the last remnant in modern man, bequeathed by primitive ancestors, of the dread and horror the hunter felt when he became the hunted.

Pete kicked his fire into a sparking blaze, pitched on more wood, dug out the pistol Sarah had nagged him about, and waited. The wolves did not attack. He didn't really expect them to. They didn't fear the pistol, and they didn't really fear the man, but they *did* fear fire.

He saw them, from time to time when a very bold, or very hungry one, glided into the range of the flickering light, slanted eyes bright with a greeny blaze, matted hair dull and filthy. He cursed them fiercely and clutched his pistol. He wouldn't have admitted to fear but he could hear its wavering pitch in his curses, and maybe the wolves also heard it, but they still circled and howled, and made clicking sounds when they snapped their teeth.

Once he hurled a firebrand into their midst and that caused consternation enough to keep them farther away for a while, and eventually they slipped away, perhaps picking up another scent, their diminishing howls making old Pete's flesh feel cold.

So he sat awake and limp for the balance of the night by his fire, angry at John Carbeau, angry at the wolves, and secretly contemptuous of his own fear, and angry at himself.

He fell asleep shortly before dawn arrived again, propped up in a cross-legged position, the pistol in his lap, the fire warming him, and the wolves gone so far off that he couldn't even have heard them if he'd been awake.

The heat awakened him, finally. The sun was behind him burning through the poncho, the wool mackinaw and the heavy woollen shirt bringing him to a sweat even in his slumber.

He awakened with a start, sweating and cramped. A tall, seam-faced old gaunt man was squatting across the fire soberly smoking a pipe and studying him. Nearby on the grass lay a doe deer, not more than a year old and field-dressed for carrying. That is, she hadn't been skinned although the musk-glands had been carefully, almost surgically, cut out of her hind legs, and the entrails had been left wherever she had fallen, which made her light to carry, and safe from musk-contamination. An old Winchester carbine was lying against her.

Pete blinked at the old man, turned to expectorate because bad fear made a sourness in a man, then he yawned, flexed his heavy arms and shoulders, and said, 'Good morning, Jacques. I was on my way to your place for breakfast. How are you?'

The black-eyed gaunt man removed his little pipe. 'I'm fine. Why didn't you come along last night? It's not much farther.'

'I was too tired. Night before last the damned rain caught me.'

'And last night it was the wolves,' said McLaughlin. 'They left tracks everywhere. I was following their sign on the way back and smelled your coals.'

Pete said casually, 'They were here.'

Jacques McLaughlin pointed. 'And you threw fire at them. Well, this time of year they are looking for fawns and caribou calves. Later on, when it gets hot maybe a few rabid ones would attack a man, but otherwise no. Anyway, rabid ones run blind; they are sick. I've killed them like that with stones. People say they are dangerous then, but it's not true. Unless you are asleep and they bite you, but otherwise they don't even know what they are doing.'

It was the kind of reassurance that didn't make a man feel better although it was supposed to. Sancroix picked up the pistol, shoved it under his mackinaw into the holster, got up with a curse because his legs were stiff, then he saw how high the sun was.

'I thought you were hunting early, but I see now it isn't long before noon.'

McLaughlin grunted upright, heaved the doe to his shoulders, retrieved his carbine and also cocked an eye at the sun. Then he stood a moment longer studying Sancroix before he stepped over the cold coals and started homeward without another word. There was something troubling his mind, and Sancroix knew it, felt it, but if McLaughlin had anything to say it was up to him to utter the first word.

They kept to the forest-fringe which skirted the flatter, open country on their right. It was cooler that way, and although spring was now losing itself in summer, thick blood did not turn thin after a long winter, as swiftly as the heat of summer replaced the chill of either winter or spring. They both felt the heat, and twice they paused to sit on a log and rest a bit. Still, McLaughlin said nothing, although he kept studying Pete Sancroix.

Sancroix carried the little doe part way, but he was not in very good physical shape, so after their second halt Jacques McLaughlin took it back across his own wide and bony shoulders.

They discussed the winter just past. Jacques had trapped a little, just to keep his hand in he said, because there was no money in pelts any more, and otherwise he had lived well enough even though a couple of times snow had reached above his doorway and he'd had to climb to the roof to push it off, lest it turn to leaden ice and threaten a cave-in.

And for a change his radio's batteries hadn't gone dead right after Christmas, so he'd kept abreast of what was happening in the world, but none of it made him want to leave the valley, he said dourly, and help in the great regeneration of the human race.

Pete laughed but McLaughlin who only rarely even smiled and never laughed aloud at all, went on talking in the same, flat tone of voice, totally unamused.

He asked about his cousin — or niece, he couldn't remember which she was — Caroline Laughlin. Also he asked about many other people down at McLean. But not once did he ask about John Carbeau, and just as they came within sight of McLaughlin's stone and log house in its forest clearing, where it faced the open valley floor northward from its rocky knoll about fifty or sixty feet above a nearby creek, it dawned on Sancroix that there were two things wrong: one, although they were lifelong friends, McLaughlin had not asked about Carbeau; two, there was a straight-standing streamer of smoke arising from the stove-pipe over McLaughlin's cabin, and since McLaughlin had been out hunting all morning, obviously, and had been many miles from his cabin during that time, he couldn't possibly have stoked up his stove to make that kind of a smoke.

But Pete let Jacques keep the initiative in their conversation, not simply because that was the polite thing to do, but also because as they got closer to the cabin he was going to find the answers anyway, without appearing objectionably nosy.

Other people did not like nosy people and Crees were no exception.

Finally, only a hundred or so yards from the cabin, McLaughlin halted, shifted the doe into a more comfortable position, handed the old carbine from his right hand to his left hand, and looked at Pete. 'I wish I hadn't found you,' he said, candidly but not with any trace of resentment. 'I thought about slipping on by, but you'd have come to the cabin anyway.'

Pete's dark eyes narrowed a little with pique, but he kept silent.

'Well, come along,' muttered McLaughlin, and started forward again.

Sancroix, still silent, but very interested now, and with black eyes darting left and right, trudged along behind his reluctant host.

They hung the doe on a high limb behind the cabin, hauled her up by means of ropes so animals wouldn't gnaw her overnight while she chilled-out thoroughly, then they wasted more time by washing off blood and doe-hair at the creek. Finally McLaughlin heaved a mighty sigh and said, 'You'll be plenty hungry and so am I. Come along.'

That was all. No warning, no appeal, not even an admonition. Not that any of those things would have deterred Peter Sancroix in any case because by now his curiosity was as big as a mountain.

4

The Mystery Man

It wasn't John Carbeau after all. In
fact it was a tall, fair young man,
thick-shouldered, deep-chested, with
very dark blue eyes and a strong
set of features, now covered with a
curly, sandy beard, whom Pete Sancroix
had never seen before in his life. But
whatever else the big-boned young man
was, he was not a Cree.

Neither was he French-Canadian;
the build was wrong, the colouring,
the features, and finally, the name
was also wrong although that could
have been open to question, names
having been cast aside or appropriated
as the occasion suggested for several
hundred years.

Jacques McLaughlin's introduction
was succinct and forthright. 'This is

Pete Sancroix. He owns the store in McLean. I found him on his way here. And that is Walter King.'

Pete shook the big young man's hand and made a kind of perfunctory smile, about as much of his curiosity having been relieved as had now been also freshly aroused. He waited for Jacques to say who Walter King was, how he happened to be here, in McLaughlin's cabin, how long he'd been staying; it was an established fact in Pete's mind that no one else knew Walter King was in the valley. Strangers, particularly this time of year, were rare, and with little else to talk about, they were invariably dissected with minute and persistent care. They never escaped detection, so Walter King was a genuine surprise to Sancroix.

But McLaughlin's face was closed down against all questions as King went about putting food on the table. He hardly even raised his black eyes when Pete spoke. Obviously, McLaughlin wished to be asked no questions and wanted not to answer any.

King was less wary, less taciturn. He asked about the roads, about weather predictions, and as Pete warmed up, as he ate, and drank bitter black coffee, they hit it off well enough. Only old Jacques sitting silent and hungry at the far end of the plank table, struck a discordant note.

Pete was careful. There was some undercurrent in the cabin. It was more than just the customary silence of a solitary man like McLaughlin, who was never very talkative at his noisiest. It was also noticeable in the way Walter King elicited information but never offered any.

Of course people, generally men, did not burst out into praise of themselves, but it seemed to Pete that this young man managed better than most, although he was amiable and talkative enough, to leave a larger blank space in their conversation than most men could have done. Unless of course they were working hard to accomplish that end.

The three of them cleaned up the dishes, and the three of them went out to skin the little doe. They even worked together in amiable co-operation at cutting firewood as the afternoon moved along, sunlight reddened and slanted, and an old cow-moose ambled by at the creek as though three men watching was something she endured every day of her life.

Finally, as they returned to the cabin, McLaughlin picked something off a wall-bunk and dropped it on the table in front of Pete. 'Give it to John when you see him again,' he said, then turned his back at the fireplace mantel while he reamed out his pipe with great care, refilled it, and lit up.

'He was here, eh?' asked Pete, and McLaughlin nodded through the pungent tobacco-smoke. Pete pocketed the pouch. 'I've been all over looking for him.'

'By now he's back at McLean,' stated Jacques, and went to a chair to sit

43

down, while Walter King worked deftly at getting dinner.

They looked at each other for a while, with Sancroix occasionally raising his eyes to watch the big young man do his work near the cook-stove. Finally Jacques put the pipe aside.

'He has been with me most of the winter.' Jacques gestured towards some cured skins stacked overhead among the log rafters. 'We trapped, hunted, went a few places. That's all.'

Pete stared at McLaughlin. All this was fine; it was about what any two men would have done, holed up in a cabin most of a bad winter. But it also left more unsaid than had been said.

Jacques understood both Sancroix's stare and his silence. He re-lit the pipe and puffed on it for a moment. 'Well, he came in on snowshoes through the mountains.'

That was interesting. Pete, having already made his physical appraisal, knew the young man was very powerful, and now wondered *why* Walter King had worked so hard to avoid the village.

But McLaughlin did not explain. In fact he went off on a new topic. 'We got some of the best martins you ever saw, Pete. And otter. It was like it used to be, until warm weather came. You know, when I was a young man a catch like that would have brought a man enough money to live all year without raising his hand.'

Walter King, listening of course, raised his dark blue eyes and took Sancroix's measure in total silence, then returned to work at the stove. Later, he came to the table, put out the plates, the implements, and went back to the stove. One thing did not need saying: Walter King was an accomplished cook.

Sancroix went down to the creek to wash before he ate. Afterwards he stood on the spongy bank considering everything he had thus far been told, and it added up to something that made him a little uneasy.

Many years ago, when Pete had been

a lad, a few men went in and out of Portage Valley by the southward mountain passes. Now and then the remains of a few who dozed off in three feet of snow would turn up in the summertime, too.

Nowadays people used the roads, which were kept open by snowploughs most of the time. If a man, even a big, strong, young one, went to all the trouble, and peril, of snowshoeing through the passes even nowadays in order to avoid passing through the village —

'Hey, Pete.'

Sancroix turned and watched Jacques stroll along the creek-bank towards him, no longer puffing on his little pipe.

'Curiosity is eating you up, Pete.'

Sancroix still asked no question. But he said, 'In my boots it would be eating you up too.'

'Yes, I think it would. Well, I said he came in over the mountains so's you'd figure it out.'

'That's a big help,' muttered Sancroix. 'People don't even do that any more, if they don't want the police to know they are here.'

'No? Well, you couldn't drive into McLean and leave your car, could you, and come trekking out to my place, without people talking about it all winter long?'

'They talk anyway, Jacques.'

'Not about Walt, because they didn't know he was here.'

'John knows.'

McLaughlin nodded. 'He knew four months ago. He went out and met Walt on snowshoes and guided him down to my place.'

That surprised Pete, who stared. 'When? He was at the store through the winter.'

'I said Walt came in four months ago.'

Sancroix counted back in his mind, then tried to remember Carbeau's absence. It was too long ago, and there had been other things to think about. Furthermore, that wasn't entirely pertinent, so Sancroix shrugged. 'All right. Now do we go on playing this game until we see the moon come up?'

'The trouble is, Pete, it's still got to be a secret. You came along and made a mess of everything.'

Sancroix's temper was triggered by that. '*I* didn't make a mess of anything. I came looking for John. And even that wasn't my idea. People were worrying; John was gone a full week.'

'Here most of it.'

'Jacques, that doesn't make any difference. *Someone* had to make certain he wasn't sick or hurt, out here. How would I know you are hiding a murderer, or a thief, or someone like that? Messed things up! How long before a constable would come through — or someone would see King hunting — or would notice too many tracks leading to and from your cabin?'

None of this seemed to bother

McLaughlin, a man in his durable sixties to whom no peril was ever very serious because he was a complete and total fatalist.

'Pete, if you went back, and if people asked a lot of questions, what would you tell them?'

'What *should* I tell them?'

'Nothing,' replied McLaughlin without a moment's hesitation.

'All right. But they are going to want to know if I stopped here; in fact they are going to know very well I wouldn't pass by without stopping, and I'd certainly be here, because they knew I was going to drop in on everyone I could see in the search. And when the police come, and I lie, and they eventually find out — where does that leave me?'

'Walt will be gone in another few weeks. What makes you think a constable would come through before then?'

'Dammit, Jacques, if you lived closer you'd know they visit every village each

49

spring, and during summertime they come and spend the night once or twice in the season to keep track of the hunters and campers; the tourists.'

McLaughlin thought on this for a moment, drifted a steady glance towards the back of his cabin where lamplight shone from a window, then he said, 'Pete, it's John's daughter's young man.'

Pete's brows puckered. 'Josephine? You mean Josie Carbeau?'

'Yes. They are in love.'

Sancroix made a helpless little gesture with his arms, typically French. 'But how can she be in love with a thief — or whatever he is?'

'He's not a thief.'

'A murderer then. And that is worse. How did John ever let this go on, and why did you take him into — ?'

'He's not a criminal, Pete. But he *is* in trouble.'

'Yes. And it isn't a little bit of trouble, is it? Or John wouldn't have met him in the pass and snuck him out here for you to hide all winter.'

'Pete, that's not our affair. All I wish is that I hadn't found you out here. I'm afraid when you return you'll make a slip and people will know he's here.'

'Not a criminal,' mumbled Sancroix. 'Not a thief or a murderer. Do you want my advice, Jacques? Get him out of here today, no later than tomorrow, and don't be mixed up in this.'

'He's already paid me to stay six months.'

'Ahh? Paid you? No, of course he's not a thief. Well, give it back and make him leave.'

McLaughlin's black gaze was thoughtfully on Sancroix. 'He wouldn't get a mile — two miles — this time of year without berry-gatherers or hunters sighting him. He knows the country only for a few miles around the cabin. Otherwise, without snow now, it would all look different and he'd get lost.'

'You'll be lost too, if the police come, Jacques.'

'I told you. It's not a police matter.'

'Hah! What else can a man fear so much he has to hide in a place like this, Jacques? An angry wife, a betrayed husband? I don't believe it, that he's not a criminal.'

'Promise me, Pete, that when you get back you won't mention seeing me or him.'

Sancroix didn't hesitate at all. 'All right. And so now I am an accessory also.'

'A what?'

'You went to school right alongside me, Jacques, don't pretend you don't know what that word means. It means that when the police come and ask, and I lie to them, then I'm guilty of helping a criminal, and that makes me equally guilty.'

'Pete, if I give you my word he's not in trouble with the law, will you believe me?'

Sancroix was stopped cold. McLaughlin would not lie. It wasn't just that the Crees did not lie, but around the countryside it was rare to find anyone who lied. There was no need, really. But now it was different, now there was something to be concealed, and that might make a difference.

But as Sancroix made his decision and said he would take McLaughlin's word, he also made a little reservation; the moment he arrived back in the village he was going to find John Carbeau and find out just exactly what all this was about.

Walt King called to them from the cabin that dinner was ready.

'You go in the morning,' said Jacques.

Pete retorted that he would be glad to go in the morning. He also said, 'How long have I known you, Jacques? But you don't trust me. I'm going to remember that.'

5

Back Home

Pete left right after breakfast the following morning without really achieving any sense of personal satisfaction even though he had sat up until nine o'clock the night before with Jacques and Walter King, talking.

It was amazing, the way King could carry on a lengthy conversation, even be amusing, and never say anything that gave a clue about himself. It was also frustrating.

There was some consolation on the trail, for when Pete paused shortly after high noon to squat by a creek and eat some of the food Walter King had wrapped for him to take along, Pete had to re-aver that the big young man was unequalled as a cook.

It wasn't altogether the cooking,

either. A lot of people, Sarah for instance, could broil a venison steak until it could compete very well with choice beef. But how many people could make a stiff sauce to go with the venison out of mushrooms, cheese and spice? And how many would remember to put a little of that sauce in a packet of food someone was to eat on the trail?

Undoubtedly Walter King had worked in some prison kitchen where he'd had the time to experiment. Men were never born with such ability, and why should they otherwise wish to develop it? Unless . . .

Pete Sancroix passed one of his former camps with the sun still high, and pressed onward. Apart from feeling more motivated now, he was eager to get back and buttonhole John Carbeau.

He spent one night out. It was of course unavoidable. In a flat country without any obstacles it was indeed a poor trekker who couldn't walk seven miles in one day; in less than one full day in fact. But this was neither flat country nor free of obstacles.

But it was an uneventful night. No rain or cold or wolves, or even any particular inner turmoils, although as he sat eating the last of his packet of food, he had some tough and pithy thoughts about Jacques McLaughlin; they had known each other a good many years. There had never been any reason for mistrust between them. And now a stranger had come along and all that was changed.

And that also applied to his lifelong friend John Carbeau. Jacques had said John had known of King's presence all those months, and although John had hung around the store, had talked of everything under the sun during that time, he had declined to take his old friend into his confidence.

The following morning Sancroix was on the trail an hour ahead of sunrise. By the time the sun was high and warm he had only one great curve of forested land up ahead to cut around, then he would be able to see the village.

For breakfast he had a long drink of icy water from a brawling little white-water creek, and although he could very easily have caught a trout in the shallows of that place and cooked it, he didn't bother. Trekking, as anyone knew, was best done on an empty stomach.

By the time he saw McLean, with smoke still rising from a few tin stovepipes, the heat was noticeable in open glades. Once, there had been a log fort a mile or so above the village. It had long ago rotted to the ground, but there remained a mound of soft silt and some punky old bits of powdery wood to mark the site. He stopped there for a moment to consider the village. Not for any particular reason except that now, for an obvious reason, he felt like a conspirator. Old Jacques had laid that obligation upon him.

There were several cars on the main thoroughfare, as usually was the case in summertime. Wintertime people had no place to go in a car they couldn't reach better on foot, so the cars remained in sheds. But summertime was different.

But what Sancroix was interested in was whether any of those vehicles were strange to him, and when he felt sure he recognized each one, he continued on down towards town.

He probably should have gone first to the store so that Sarah would be relieved, but instead he went home, shed the poncho, the light pack he'd carried with its blankets, and even put on a lighter pair of boots. He also left the flares and the pistol at home. Then he went on down to John Carbeau's place, but no one was about, so finally he went to the store.

John was not there, but Sarah was and she greeted him with a reserved kiss and an expression of relief. Then she said, 'John came back yesterday. I told him we were worried and that you had gone looking for him.'

Pete was curious. 'What did he say?'

'Nothing much. Only that you would have a wild goose chase.' Sarah's fine dark eyes were steady. 'Did you?'

Pete nodded. He had never had occasion to lie to his wife so he couldn't quite bring himself to do it now. 'Not only that,' he muttered, 'but there were wolves — and the first — or was it the second? — night, I got soaked when it rained.' He glanced around. The store had no customers at the moment. 'Was John here today?' he asked.

Sarah nodded. 'For a little while this morning.' Her face softened slightly. 'It's summertime, Pete. He won't be around much from now on.'

'I want to see him.'

Sarah studied her man. 'What about?'

Pete's exasperation came out. 'What about! About making me go hiking all over hell's half-acre for nothing, that's what about! And I told you and Trudeau he was all right, but no, you had to make me feel like I was being cruel — so I could have caught pneumonia in the rain or been bitten by a wolf — and for nothing.'

Sarah smiled. Pete's temper, much

improved over the years, was more likely to turn to petulance now than to burn with real animosity. 'Go in the back room,' she said. 'I heated some soup for lunch. It will still be warm. And there is coffee.'

Pete went, but Sarah remained behind in the store. She had already had her noon-day meal, and anyway, apart from the possibility that a customer might walk in, Pete wouldn't be very good company until he got over his irritability.

She did, in fact, have customers. Business was often quite brisk in summertime. The native villagers who sustained the store in wintertime still came in, but what made trade especially lucrative in the warm, snow-free months was vacationers.

There were a few Americans, but mostly the vacationers were people from Quebec or Montreal. It was always hopefully said that one of these days the Americans would 'discover' Portage Valley, and would come in droves; of course when that happened everyone would benefit because the American-vacationer was the only person who always had plenty of money to spend.

John Carbeau came drifting back to the store about three in the afternoon. By that time Sarah had gone home to take care of her own work, and Pete was back where he properly belonged, behind his counters and among his laden shelves.

There were two women buying bolt-goods when John strolled in, so Pete couldn't rush right over and confront him. Usually, Pete had patience with women shoppers but this afternoon he had to force himself to be that way.

Still, Carbeau went to the stove and sat in one of the old captain's chairs the way he usually did, even though the stove hadn't been stoked since the heat outside got warm enough to make additional heat unnecessary. Evidently John was not going anywhere.

To heap coals upon Pete's exasperation, he had no sooner got rid of the two women, than several young men came in dressed in the painfully new red coats and heavy woollen shirts, not to mention sleekly oiled Bean boots, that marked the holiday-maker, and wished to lay in a supply of tinned goods.

Normally, this was the kind of trade Pete throve on. He could even hoist a few prices, although being careful not to overdo it, because unless people patronized his establishment, they would have to turn back to the next nearest town southward, which was a long drive, to stock up.

John sat by the cool stove blandly considering the newcomers, and it never once dawned upon Pete Sancroix that Carbeau could be just as curious about what Pete had learned on his trek, as Pete was about John's knowledge of the Walter King matter.

Eventually Pete got rid of the young men, who had told him they had made a camp up near one of the inland lakes, had put away the money from them, and because he was afraid someone else might come into the store, even though it was past four o'clock in the afternoon by this time, Pete crossed to where John sat and scowled darkly.

'Well?' he demanded.

John's imperturbable gaze lifted and lingered. 'You went to Jacques's place?'

'Of course I went there. That's where I'd expect to find you.'

'Yes,' conceded Carbeau, and fell to searching diligently for a hangnail. 'And you spent a night there?'

Pete Sancroix put both hands on his hips. 'Damn it you know I'd spend the night there. And ate there. So what is the point of all this pussy-footing? Who *is* he, and why did you risk your neck bringing him through the mountains? Why is he hiding out there, and what were you thinking of to get Jacques involved?'

Carbeau abandoned the hangnail search. 'I didn't mean to cause you all that discomfort, Pete. Sarah told me — even when Trudeau said I might be hurt out there — you told him I could always manage to — '

'Never mind,' exclaimed Pete Sancroix. 'Who is that young man out there? Why is he hiding?'

'Josie sent him up last autumn.'

'Go on. What has he done?'

'He's not a criminal, Pete.'

'No, of course not. He hides up here because, well, because he is a spy for the C.I.A. and the Chinese are looking for him.' Pete made a great grunt, kicked a chair around and dropped down. 'John, do you understand you can get us all in trouble about this? Not just Jacques, but me as well? And if Josephine is in love with this young man explain please, why he is up here and she is down in Quebec?'

'She will be here tonight.'

'She will? And how do you know that?'

'Pierre Trudeau brought a letter. It was waiting when I got back.'

'All right. Josephine will drive in tonight. But John, I still want to know why Walter King has been hiding all winter. Now don't tell me he did not hide intentionally, because you, yourself, brought him in through the passes, on snowshoes, so he wouldn't be seen in the village.'

Carbeau remained bland. 'I'm not trying to tell you I didn't want him seen in McLean, Pete. I'm not telling you anything at all. It isn't my place. Wait until Josephine gets here, then, if she is willing, you ask and she will answer.'

Sancroix, recognizing he was going to have to be satisfied with that, asked just one more question. 'But you *do* John?'

'Yes. And so does Jacques. What did he tell you?'

Sancroix spat a soft curse. 'What does he ever tell anyone about anything? He has lived out there like a hermit so long he has to prime himself just to say good-morning.'

Carbeau smiled, rose and lightly lay a hand upon his old friend's shoulder.

65

'*Ami voyageur*, there is only one thing I would not tell you; whatever I have sworn not to mention at all. Otherwise, you could know anything I know. And you know that, eh?'

Sancroix shoved upright out of the chair and shrugged. He was placated. Still, it had been an unpleasant trek, particularly that blasted rain and those confounded wolves. He said, 'What time does Josie arrive this evening?'

John didn't know. He dug out the letter to show Pete where it said the time of day she would depart from Quebec, not the time she would arrive at McLean, and that was understandable because in spring and winter progress depended entirely upon the condition of the road, while in summertime there were other considerations, all tending to make a traveller wary of trying to adhere to a schedule.

'Come by the house after supper,' Carbeau said, putting up the letter and heading for the front door. 'And you are sure Jacques told you nothing?'

Pete raised a stiff arm. 'Get out. Go on home!'

Normally he'd have had a twinge of remorse for using that kind of language to an old friend, but Carbeau's parting question had re-aroused all Sancroix's irritability all over again.

Later, after he'd locked the store and trudged home for dinner, he told Sarah he had to go see John later, and offered no explanation. She didn't ask for one. She didn't even expect one. She was a very exceptional wife, indeed.

He *did* tell her Josie Carbeau was arriving tonight, and that interested her very much. Josephine Carbeau was about the same age as her own daughters, who were married and gone now too; Josie had spent almost as much time at the Sancroix place as she'd spent in her own home. Sarah had tried very hard to be a second mother to Josie, and in the process had come to love John Cardeau's daughter as though she were her own child.

'Then I'll go over there with you,' said Sarah, and was surprised at the look she got as her man rose and went stamping after his mackinaw.

'You'll do no such a thing! You'll stay right here!'

6

A Secret is Revealed

Josephine Carbeau was five feet and six inches tall, and probably weighed in the neighbourhood of one hundred and thirty-five pounds.

She was long-limbed, creamy-skinned, jet-haired and dark-eyed. Her features were perfect. In a word, Josephine Carbeau was exquisite, and that meant she was exquisite when she was calm and serene. But when she was angry, as Pete Sancroix had occasion to tell Sarah much later, she was able to take away a person's breath.

And she was angry when, shortly after her arrival at her father's house, Pete Sancroix struck his palm with a balled fist and demanded to know what kind of wretched deceit she was perpetrating upon McLean and all the people who had been aunts and uncles to her, by sneaking that criminal into Portage Valley and concealing him out at McLaughlin's place.

Afterwards, when her father had calmed her down, she went over and kissed Pete's leathery cheek and said, 'Please . . . I've been driving most of the day, I was a little wrought up and nervous, and tired. I apologize.'

Pete and John exchanged a dark-eyed look and Pete shrugged. She'd told him to mind his own business and some other things, but she hadn't *sworn* at him, or impugned either the species of his mother nor his own legitimacy, and anyway it was obvious from the dark places beneath her beautiful soft eyes, that she'd been under a recent strain, so Pete clumsily patted her shoulder and said that if John had coffee maybe they should all go into the kitchen and have a cup.

It was a good suggestion. Josephine went to shed her jacket, her white blouse, slip into a thick old baggy white sweater and some heelless shoes, then joined them as the coffee spread its wonderful aroma throughout the large, comfortable old cabin.

She first wished to know how Pete had discovered that Walter existed. He explained about that, not failing to mention the bitter rainfall one night, and the wolves.

Then Josephine said, 'We are going to be married in a month.'

Pete held forth the cup for John to pour it full. 'All right,' he conceded. 'You will be married. But what of the police, child, and the heartache and the — ?'

'Police?' she murmured, gazing from Pete to her father. 'Has he done something here?'

John explained. 'Pete is convinced your young man is some kind of criminal hiding from the law.'

Josephine looked big-eyed at them. Her father resumed his place at the kitchen table, and when she started to say something spirited old John held up a hand. 'Wait. You made me promise to keep your secret. I kept it. Neither Jacques nor I told a single soul. But now that you are here, and now that Pete knows part of it, why then it's up to you what else to tell him. It never was up to me.'

Josephine shot Sancroix a look, and was apologetic again. 'I didn't mean they couldn't have told *you*. What I meant was that they shouldn't let *everyone* know.'

Pete's brows arched. 'How do you tell some people something and not have all people know it within a very short period of time? Especially here in this town?'

Josephine smiled. It was an expression that would have melted a perma-frost encased in stone. 'Uncle Pete, Walter has broken no laws. I love him very much and he loves me, but we can't be married until the end of next month, you see, so — '

'Wait. I *don't* see.'

'Uncle Pete, have you ever heard of

the King Syndicate of New York?'

'No.'

'It is a very old rich American amalgam.'

'An American what?'

'Uncle Pete, the Kings started out with buggy shops two hundred years ago. Then they branched out into shipping and importing, into sugar and oil and transportation. It is the most diversified financial syndicate in the States.'

'I see. Go on.'

'Walter and one brother are the sole heirs. Their father died some years back and their grandfather, who had been retired, came back to head the company. He had both boys, Walter King and Sanford King, educated in law. Then he sent them to Europe for practical experience among the subsidiary companies over there, and last year he brought Walter home and pushed him into a skyscraper office with orders to take charge of the transportation subsidiary concerns.'

Pete nodded his head. He had no trouble following the gist of all this at all, but some of the words Josie used skimmed overhead without his even trying to understand them.

'Walter will inherit from his father at the end of this month. I met him when he visited Quebec last year. He came back three times after that, until his grandfather sent a man up here to offer me a hundred thousand dollars never to see him again. I refused, and when I told Walter he went to see his grandfather. There was a terrible argument. His grandfather said he would see to it that we would never see each other again if it cost him a million dollars. He then ordered Walter back to Europe.'

Pete finally leaned back in his chair and relaxed. It was all at last beginning to assume some kind of order in his mind.

'He didn't go to Europe. He came back to Quebec. I wrote my father. Between us we worked out this scheme and you know the rest.'

John Carbeau nodded slowly. 'I met him on snowshoes, as you know, Pete, and I had already made arrangements for the boy to stay with Jacques. It was only supposed to be for one more month. After that they could be married.'

'I don't understand that part,' confessed Pete Sancroix. 'You said he will inherit money in another month. Is that it? The pair of you wish to be sure of the money first?'

Josephine gave her head a violent shake. 'I'd marry him tomorrow. In his father's will it says that unless he is still unmarried on his twenty-ninth birthday, he is not to participate in the estate. He refuses to marry me until his twenty-ninth birthday.'

'I see. Then for *him* it is the money, but not for you?'

Josephine's dark eyes were soft-sad and shadowed. 'I told you, Uncle Pete. I'd have married him last year. He says he has been punished and shunted here and there all his life by the syndicate; that he earned that money before he'd finished elementary school, and now, because his grandfather is so dead set against him marrying at all, he's going to be married one day after his birthday, then claim the ten million dollars.'

Pete gently let all his breath out, then just as gently refilled his lungs. 'Ten million dollars,' he whispered.

'I don't care about that money,' exclaimed Josephine.

At once Pete raised an admonishing hand in the manner of a man who had just heard hair-raising blasphemy. 'Wait, Josie. Now be a sensible girl. You want the young man, yes? All right; then for one more month he hides from his grandfather out at the McLaughlin place. Fine. After that, you marry him right here in the village — and he inherits the money. Now listen to me, child, I'm going to tell you something you should always remember. Money cannot buy happiness, as they say.

That is indeed true. But Josephine, you can be much happier *with* ten million dollars, than you can ever be *without* it.'

John was stuffing shag into his little pipe when Sancroix said that. For a moment John looked at the other, older man, then wordlessly resumed stuffing his pipe. Whether he agreed, disagreed, or was merely amused at Sancroix's shocked reaction to Josie's denunciation of wealth, went unexplained.

But when John had the pipe going, he said, 'Josie, something I have never been able to figure out. When I was twenty-nine years old, I was making my own way, and no one could have made me go somewhere to hide.'

Josie sighed. 'Dad, you don't *know* Everett King, Walter's grandfather. Why, even in the newspapers they call him the old autocrat, the old dictator, things like that. Everyone fears him. If you knew him you'd realize what a courageous thing Walter has done.'

Pete was less concerned with this

than he was with something else. 'Josie, in the four months since Walter King came here, if his grandfather is so powerful, why hasn't he hired men to find Walter?'

Josephine smiled a trifle harshly. 'Uncle Pete, he's had men watching me day and night, thinking I'd lead them to Walter. So I haven't left Quebec, not even once, until this morning. You see, his grandfather doesn't really know which way Walter went, or whether he is still even seeing me. It's been a strain, but this is how we planned it. Once, I heard from Sanford that Grandfather King got a tip that Walter was in Paris, and sent three men to find him. Uncle Pete, unless I lead them to Walter — or unless you or Dad, or Jacques does that — they aren't going to find him.'

'But you are here now,' said Pete, straightening up slightly in his chair.

'This is my home. They already know that. I shouldn't have come, but I had to. Anyway, this is as far as I'll lead them, do you see? I won't go to see Walter. Then, in a few days when I go back, all they'll be able to report to Mr Everett King is that I visited my father at McLean.'

That left Pete worried and unconvinced. 'Just this afternoon three strangers came to the store,' he told her, and her father, who had studied those three closely, nodded as though he hadn't fogotten those men. 'Maybe they were vacationers like they said, Josie, but who can tell? Now tell me, did you see a car following you, or something like that?'

She smiled and shook her head. 'You don't see these men, Uncle Pete. They aren't the kind that play cops-and-robbers. Mr. King wouldn't hire men like that. No, I wasn't followed. At least I tried to see them at it and never did. But after a year of living like some kind of fugitive in Quebec, I got to know the *feeling* of being watched. They will have reported to Mr King that I'm here, and they will be here too.'

Pete spread his thick arms wide. 'In McLean no one arrives without being noticed. In the store I hear of every stranger. I'll know within a day or two who they are.'

John puffed and said, 'The important thing, Pete, is that they don't find Jacques's cabin.'

Sancroix nodded over that, and all the animus he'd shown earlier towards both Josephine and her father, was completely obliterated from his mind. He did not think of his recent and unpleasant trek, but if he had, it now would have appeared to him as something self-sacrificing and noble.

'They won't,' he told John. 'Only four of us know, and none of us will tell. But Josie, if you stay here very long those men may begin to look around; maybe to wonder about those isolated cabins and to ask questions. If you stay and they feel they have the time, those men may even start hiking around the valley.'

'I'll leave in a couple of days,' said

the beautiful girl, and rose from the table to smile at the older men. 'I just don't know what I'd do without both of you,' and while they looked awkwardly away, she told them she was very tired, and left the kitchen.

For a while John smoked and sat silent, while Pete Sancroix's broad brow was furrowed in hard thought. After a while John said, 'Well, that is the story. And now you understand. It was *her* secret, not mine. But even if it had been just my secret — the fewer people who know things, the less chance of someone accidentally saying something.'

Pete was far beyond that consideration by now. He was worrying about these strangers this old man Everett King would have nosing around. It still seemed reasonable to him that they just might find McLaughlin's cabin.

'Well, I think we've got to get her to go away quickly, and we've got to find out where these men are and make very sure that they don't go hiking out in the valley.'

On that note the meeting broke up. John offered his friend a drink of scotch, but Pete declined and went trudging home. It didn't occur to him until he saw the light in the parlour window that Sarah would be waiting up with that questioning look in her eyes.

He stood outside for ten minutes wrestling with an awkward lie he tried to fabricate, then gave it up because it not only didn't sound reasonable, but because he choked on the idea of lying to her, and walked indoors to be obdurate, so she would become angry, and they would go to bed not speaking to one another.

And that is exactly how it happened, too.

7

A Nearing Crisis

As Sancroix was to tell John Carbeau the following winter when all this trouble was behind them, secrets were not really supposed to be kept.

What happened was the same thing that invariably happens with secrets. The more adamant those who knew Josephine's secret were about keeping it, the more inevitable it became that someone should stumble over it

How that happened was unique, in one sense, and very understandable in another sense. Caroline Laughlin, Jacques McLaughlin's niece, took full advantage of the splendid summertime weather to trek out and see how her uncle had wintered.

She met Walter King.

There was no way for it to be

avoided, and in fact if it hadn't been Caroline it would have been someone else, because now that all restrictions had been removed, people went fishing or hunting, or just berry-picking, but in any case they fanned out with pleasure, even laughter, over Portage Valley.

Jacques's cabin was not athwart any travelled trails, but still, as John lugubriously told Pete Sancroix when Caroline returned to announce that to her complete surprise, a fair and very handsome young man had wintered out there with her uncle, the cabin was accessible.

If it had been possible for John or Pete to meet Caroline first, before she'd broadcast her astonishment all over town, perhaps the secret might still have survived, although after Sarah heard the whole story from her man, she scorned that idea.

'Caroline Laughlin has a mouth that runs over from both sides, and always has.'

Sarah left the store, where her man

had first heard the news from someone who had heard it from Caroline, and hastened over to the Carbeau house to be with Josephine.

Only a little later John walked in. He had also heard the talk, but instead of being confined to a store where he could only stand and fume like Sancroix was doing, John Carbeau had arrived at a decision.

'I'll go out there tonight,' he told Pete, 'after dark, and by breakfast time I will find them and explain why Walter has to go.'

Pete gave his thick arms a great flap. 'Go where?'

'Well, I'll try and smuggle him back here late tomorrow night, if we can get along fast enough. Then he and Josie can decide.'

John ceased speaking as two stalwart strangers in those glaringly new boots and hats and jackets entered the store. Both he and Pete stood statue-like watching the newcomers.

The strangers were not exactly young

men; perhaps they were both in their forties. But they were physically fit and capable-enough appearing, except that their faces were pale, as though they spent very little time out of doors.

They were pleasant men, and courteous, making certain first that they were not interrupting John and Pete before handing Sancroix a list of their needs, and looking a little abashed as they frankly said they were the worst kind of tenderfeet, but had decided to try camping out somewhere up in the valley for a few days, just so they wouldn't have to smell a car or see another human face, or listen to city-noises.

They said they were from Boston and showed non-resident angling permits when Pete discreetly enquired, as he began assembling some of the fishing lures they had on their list.

They even offered to hire John as a guide, but he smilingly, and wordlessly, declined, and went over by the stove until the men had departed. Afterwards, he and Pete stared out of a streaked front window as the strangers climbed into a four-wheel-drive Land Rover and went northward out of the village.

'Now I've got to get out there tonight,' exclaimed John. 'If it isn't those two, then it will be others.'

Sancroix did not dispute that at all. He nodded his head in agreement, but for one thing. 'Listen; if you bring the lad here, John, it's going to double the risk for him.'

'Yes. And if I *don't* bring him here, my daughter will look even more forlorn and demoralized than she looks now. What would you do?'

Sancroix looked around at his shelves of tinned goods. 'What will you need?'

After Carbeau had left the store Pete had customers until shortly before closing time, but all were known to him. When he closed up a little early and stood out on the sidewalk for a moment considering the bright, pale sky — it wouldn't even start getting dark until nine o'clock — he wondered if, after all, those two large men, those strangers, were either as innocent as they acted, or were as inexperienced at tracking someone while there was still daylight.'

When he got home he found Josephine helping his wife make dinner, and that pleased him although he hadn't thought of her being alone at the Carbeau place until he saw her with Sarah.

If Josephine was worried she didn't show it, and that made Pete wonder if her father had mentioned the two large men who had entered the store. Probably he hadn't; it would only have heightened Josephine's tensions and maybe those men were nothing more than they claimed to be.

Pete mixed a drink in the kitchen under Sarah's dark and watching eye, and was jovial. That made his wife look a little wryly at him too. He said there were times when no matter what a man did, it did not please a woman.

Sarah arched her brows but said

nothing, and Josephine smiled gently as she told him she couldn't recall a single time when he hadn't managed to please her. Then she surprised him by saying, 'Those men who came to the store this afternoon, Uncle Pete, probably weren't the ones.'

He muttered something and took a long pull of his drink to recover from the shock of being proved wrong. Then he moved his shoulders as though those men had never been a secret anyway, and pulled out a chair from the kitchen table to sit down.

'The trouble is that this time of year it might be hard to tell. I heard of a solitary camper with some cameras over near the westerly passes trying to get photographs of bears.'

Sarah didn't think that was very clever. 'A man by himself going after bears, even with a gun, isn't very safe.'

'And there is a party, with women and children, over at one of the easterly lakes,' went on Pete. 'I heard that from

Pierre Trudeau. They sent a man back to the road to flag him down because their car got stuck in some muskeg. Trudeau had to go to pull them out with his powerwagon.'

Josephine said it was not impossible that the men Mr King would send, might bring along women and children, but she doubted it.

Sarah was interested in Mr King, not the men he would send. She asked if Josie had ever talked to the old man.

She had, twice. Once when Walter took her to meet him down in New York, and again over the telephone when he'd called her in Quebec after she'd turned down the hundred-thousand-dollar bribe. The last time, Josie said, he was very disagreeable, and the first time he was just himself — which was slightly disagreeable.

They laughed a little about that, but Sarah clung to the subject. 'He can't be reasoned with at all? I've never met such a person.'

'Aunt Sarah, you've never met two hundred and fifty million dollars. It isn't a man, it's a syndicated empire that jerks the strings for a withered old juiceless man who has the two hundred and fifty million dollars.'

'What good are his grandsons unmarried?' Sarah wanted to know. 'What good is *any* man without a woman?'

Pete swished his drink, said nothing, and thought about that with the chair tilted back. Josephine simply shook her head. She had no answer either, even though she was also doing some private thinking.

'I'd like to see this old man,' Sarah said, as though Everett King were just another human being, and of course he was anything but that.

Josephine could have explained, but she didn't. They were ready to put the food on the table which was a diversion, so the topic of Everett King was dropped, except for one last salvo fired by Sarah.

'What will happen when this old man learns that his grandson has been hiding up here all winter? If he is anything like you say, Josie, he will be mad at Jacques.'

That was a startling thought. In the course of all the recent discussions no one had brought up anything like this before, so now, as Pete Sancroix hitched his chair closer to the table, it bothered him. What Josephine said next also bothered him.

'I don't know what I was thinking of when I encouraged Walt and my father to adopt this scheme. It didn't even occur to me until after I'd talked to Sanford on the telephone, that Mr King might feel vindictive towards anyone who helped.'

Sarah heaped her husband's plate, set it before him and gave him her softest, dark-eyed look. 'Pete, what is a little trouble, eh?'

Sancroix showed a brave smile. 'What can he do to Jacques — or to any of us?'

Sarah nodded, sat across from her man and started eating. She alone of the three of them had no very clear idea of what someone with two hundred and fifty million dollars could do, if they set their minds to it. In her calm innocence she was scornful, and that made her husband wince.

But on the other hand, when he looked at lovely Josie, everything gallically gallant arose in his breast. 'Well,' he summarized for them, 'whatever he does had better be soon.' The women looked over at him. He smiled back. 'There are only a few more days left in this month, and next month will pass very swiftly, eh?'

After dinner they went to check television reception in the big old parlour. Usually this time of year it was good, unless of course some of those local electrical storms were coming out of the far north, which sometimes interfered so badly it was useless to keep a set switched on.

As they were getting comfortable

Josie said, 'You don't suppose Mr King's men will also be watching my father, do you, Uncle Pete?'

Sancroix hadn't considered that, but as he did so now he had to smile. 'Mr King could only hire one man who could track your father, and that is your father himself. No, I wouldn't worry. Not about that.' Pete gazed at the girl a long moment then said, 'But if you need something to worry about, give some thought to what happens after your father brings the young man here tomorrow night — and after that, what must be done to hide him.'

It did not occur to Pete to doubt, after all the other things that had been said showing how much Josephine knew, that she would *not* know her father was going to return with Walter King.

But as her face drained of colour and her eyes got perfectly round, both he and his wife saw that he had indeed, dropped a clanger.

'He can't,' whispered Josephine. 'He

can't possibly bring Walter to McLean. They'll see him.'

Sarah leaned to place a hand upon the girl's arm and say soothingly, 'Not at night, Josie, and not if someone meets them outside the village and takes them somewhere Mr King's men wouldn't find him in a thousand years.'

Pete, trying to reinstate himself, nodded vigorously in approval of his wife's suggestion. 'That is it, Josie.'

The girl would not be placated. 'I tell you, they will find him.'

Sarah's dark gaze hardened a trifle. 'Not on your life they won't. I'll see to that myself. But Josie, you'll have to think of what comes afterwards, because there is one thing I'm pretty certain of — we couldn't hide your young man here in McLean. They certainly *would* find him then.'

Pete scowled, still standing with a finger poised over the television switch. 'Josephine, tell me something. What if this old man's people *do* find your young man? They can't kidnap him;

they can't use guns on him here in Canada as perhaps they would dare do down in the States. And if he is twenty-nine years old, what's to stop him from looking them right in the eye and telling them to go to hell?'

Josephine slowly and sadly shook her head. 'You don't understand, Uncle Pete. You've never met men like the ones Mr King would hire for this. No one in McLean has ever had to deal with such men. They'll take Walter back to New York with them, and they'll make certain that he never gets to see me again. You just don't understand the kind of men I'm talking about.'

8

A Proposition

Pete Sancroix walked Josephine home that night, then returned to have a coffee-nightcap in the kitchen with Sarah. She was of the opinion that, as Pete had said, no one could find John Carbeau if he chose not to be found. But she was also of the opinion that Pete should hike out a mile or so the forthcoming evening, find John and keep him out of town until it was fully dark, because while it was quite possible that he couldn't return to the village before dark, someone had better make certain.

Pete agreed to go. The store would be closed by then anyway. But he was not as worried about John and Walter King, as he was about the identity of the men Mr King had in the vicinity.

It was very frustrating trying to imagine which group was them.

Sarah said not to worry because if they could help John and Josie tonight, by morning Walter King would be gone anyway.

Pete retired with Sarah's reassurances and his own misgivings, and the following morning he rose the same way. As he was leaving the house after breakfast to open the store he suggested that if Sarah had finished her housework and had nothing else to do, she might come to the store.

It was a beautiful morning. The air was fresh with pine-sap scent, the sky was laced with far-spaced little puffy clouds; if a man stepped into the street he could see two hundred miles as easily as he could normally see fifty miles.

People were moving, being noisy, responding in a dozen different ways to the magic of the day. Pete left the doorway when his first customer of the day arrived, and despite the burden he was saddled with, managed to joke a little.

It was that kind of a day. People laughed easily and smiled often. The temperature climbed until the last hold-out wearing wool had to retreat to the shade and pant.

It wasn't really good fishing weather, but only the local people knew that. Holidayers flocking into Pete's place for fresh lures and bottled bait were certain a nice, clear, hot day would bring the fish to the top by the score.

Pete sold them whatever they desired. His stock in trade was a large and varied inventory, not advice. But the hotter the weather became the deeper trout went in search of relief. Furthermore, they fed at dawn and not until after sunset, in mid-summer, very rarely leaving the shadowy, cold depth to rise for a fly or bait. And finally, on sunshiny hot days anglers cast their shadows upon the water, which alerted trout to danger.

Still, although Pete knew these and many other things about fishing, he did not consider himself much of an angler, and by local standards he wasn't; it was hard even to get away those times he and John Carbeau slipped off once or twice each summer.

When pressed for advice Pete would look about the store, and if he saw a native idling in the place or shopping, he'd send the holidayer over to the native. Occasionally this resulted in a happy relationship. If the holidayer was earnestly seeking good fishing, he would need a local guide. As soon as the rate of pay was worked out, the pair usually departed happily together.

Those two large men returned the day following their first appearance asking about a guide. They had trekked to a couple of small lakes not very far off, easterly out into the valley, and had found no fish.

There was an excellent reason for that, of course; every lake that was easily accessible had been fished-out years before. Pete explained, and while he was doing it he was thinking that if these two large men were Mr King's hirelings, they had gone in the wrong direction to find Walter King, because the McLaughlin cabin was westerly. A little north, but mostly westward.

It dawned upon him that those two big men just might not be anything other than they seemed to be. That thought didn't appease Pete's anxiety very much, because if these two weren't the ones, then who was, among the parties of vacationers beginning to flock in each day?

That afternoon, not very long after lunchtime, Pierre Trudeau arrived with a heavy mail sack — not that letter-writing had increased all that much, but because it was time for summer and autumn mail-order catalogues to start arriving.

Trudeau had an interesting scrap of information. While he was offering it Sarah came in to listen too. Pierre had met some vacationers south of town trying to make sense out of a map of Portage Valley. They had circled an area east of McLean with pencil and said they had tramped over that part and were interested now in the westerly regions.

Trudeau had explained there were no worthwhile lakes to the west until one had hiked about ten miles. Otherwise there was only creek-fishing. He told Pete and Sarah the reason he had assumed that the men were fishermen was because they had poles and tackle-boxes on the rear seat of their Land Rover.

Pete leaned upon the counter. 'Pierre, were there two of them, and were they large men, pale in the face but strong-looking?'

Trudeau considered briefly, then nodded. 'In their forties. City-men, but not as helpless-acting as most city men, if you know what I mean.'

Pete straightened up off the counter and turned to his wife. 'I'll be back in a little while.' He jerked his head at Trudeau and led the mystified postman out upon the sidewalk where he began a slow advance northward, looking along both sides of the street until he saw the Land Rover he was seeking.

'That one?' he asked Pierre, pointing.

Trudeau nodded. 'The same one. What's it all about?'

One of the big men came strolling forth from a café that served beer. Pete pointed him out too, and again Trudeau nodded.

'What have they done, Pete?'

Sancroix turned back, dragging the postman along with him. 'Nothing. Nothing at all. I was just curious.'

Trudeau said nothing but kept his perplexed look right up until he halted in front of the store, and catching hold of Pete, halted him too. 'You don't get this excited over nothing,' he said. 'If they stole from the store all you have to do is — '

'What a foolish thing to say. Look at them. Do they look like men who would steal?'

'Well, *something* is bothering you,

Pete, and it has to do with those two men.'

'Pierre, did they tell you they were going into the west end of the valley?'

'No. They listened to everything I had to say about it having muskeg swamps and this time of year lots of bears, and didn't say they were going over there or not.'

Pete suddenly brightened with an inspiration. 'They will need a guide.'

Trudeau nodded. 'Probably. They wouldn't get lost. They aren't the kind to do that. But they won't find the good fishing places without a guide, either.'

Pete smiled, clapped Trudeau on the shoulder and ducked inside the store leaving the postman standing out there in sunshine looking perplexedly after him. Trudeau eventually went out to his truck and drove away. He was still mystified, but after so many years of adhering to his mail-delivery schedule, even a genuine mystery couldn't have deterred him much longer. And he wasn't sure there *was* a mystery; it might only be that Peter Sancroix was falling victim to 'cabin-fever' as it was called, meaning the variety of claustrophobia that occasionally hit people who lived in one place too long. It wasn't too likely; after all Sancroix had spent nearly all his life at McLean, but Trudeau was at a loss otherwise to explain how Sancroix had been acting.

But Trudeau would be back again the next day, and the day after that; he could observe Sancroix and perhaps arrive at some kind of decision without having to press Sancroix for an explanation. He was sure that if he'd followed Pete into the store insisting on that explanation, he wouldn't have got it anyway.

But Sarah knew better than to suspect cabin-fever when her man returned in a rush for his hat, then rushed back outside again. She wasn't worried because Pete had been wearing his pleased and crafty look. She *was* curious, but that would be resolved in time; it always was.

When Sancroix got up the road and across to where the Land Rover had been parked the two large men were climbing in, but with no trace of haste. They seemed lethargic, but then it was that time of year. People used to long, cold winters lost most of their enthusiasm when mid-summer arrived.

One of the strangers recognized Sancroix and threw him a little wave. It was all Pete needed to amble on up and, eyeing the fishing and camping equipment in the back of the little car, smilingly to say, 'Well, by now you've discovered every creek and lake that can be walked to from the village within an hour or two, is fished out, eh?'

One of the large men considered Pete with a pair of tan eyes and nodded. 'They tell us we've got to go west quite a distance to catch anything this time of year.'

Pete meditated. 'North,' he said,

speaking with quiet and firm authority. 'That's what they tell everyone in mid-summer. Go west to the highland lakes.' Sancroix smiled craftily. 'We all fish, here in McLean. How long would the fish last if we told everyone where to find them? No; not west. Go north out across the valley. And don't bother with the lakes. Everyone camps beside the lakes. Go north to the deep holes along the creeks. *That* is where the big trout lie, growing bigger.'

The same large man, the one with the tan eyes, smiled a little at Pete. 'You know the valley pretty well, eh?'

'I was raised here. I've fished every lake and creek within a hundred miles.'

For the first time the other large man spoke. He had blue eyes and a thick, massive jaw. 'How about all the cabins and camps — do you know them too?'

Pete nodded slowly. 'Every one. When it paid a man to trap, those people always sold their pelts through my store. I not only know the ones who live in the forests now, but I knew the ones who used to live out there, and who have since died.'

The blue-eyed man was getting interested. He offered Pete a cigar, and when it was declined he lit it himself and leaned upon the car-door to say, 'If you know them that well, I suppose you'd know if a stranger came to your town — like maybe last winter — and stayed here, eh?'

Pete smiled at the blue-eyed man without a flicker of an eyelash. That remark was all he had to know. These two *were* the ones, after all.

'Mister, most of the people here are related some way or another, even if they aren't always sure just how. But no one can come here, even to visit, without everyone else hearing about it.'

The blue-eyed man was watching Pete closely and nodding his head very gently. 'Yeah. We found that out in the café. Tell me something — do you know the trail to a cabin belonging to a man named Jacques McLaughlin?'

Sancroix's heart stopped, then went on again. 'Yes, I know the trail out there. It's a long trek and sometimes it's not easy to avoid excitement. The last time I went over that far I ran into wolves.'

'Suppose,' continued the blue-eyed man in his soft deep voice, 'we offered you two hundred and fifty dollars to guide us out there.'

Pete, usually delighted at the prospect of profit, felt a slight chill this time. Obviously, these two had asked questions, and just as obviously some loud-mouth in the café had told them about Caroline Laughlin's discovery of a stranger who had wintered with Jacques McLaughlin.

He nodded at the strangers. 'My wife can mind the store. When do you want to go — in the morning?'

'Right now,' said the blue-eyed man. 'Start out this afternoon.' He shrugged.

109

'We've got sleeping bags. If we have to sleep-out, that's all right.'

Pete kept nodding. 'All right. I'll go and get my blankets. Do you have tinned food?'

'No.'

'I'll bring a sack,' said Pete, and lifted his arm to point. 'We'll ride in your car as far north as the old fort. From there we'll walk. Now wait for me, I'll be back in ten minutes.'

'Hey,' called the blue-eyed man, smiling affably. 'Would you like the money now?'

Pete shrugged. 'When we get back,' he said, and hurried along on his way to the store.

Behind him the pair of large men sat relaxed in their car watching Pete, saying nothing until the tan-eyed man chuckled, then gave his head a slow wag.

'The kid was smart, but not smart enough. You know, in a way I kind of envy him spending a winter up here.'

The blue-eyed man said, 'You're crazy. The snow gets hip-pocket deep. You'd go ape living like these people do. Well, with any luck we'll be on our way back tomorrow — with company.'

Sancroix The Guide

It only took a moment for Pete to convince Sarah about the two strangers, and of course she agreed with Pete's scheme to lead them westerly until it got dark enough to drift southerly deeper into the forest where he could bed them down, then, when they were asleep, abandon them out there deep in the woods.

But she wanted to know what he had done with the pistol he'd taken out with him the last time. It was at home, he said, and he didn't want it anyway. She would have argued, but he went after a sack, then began pitching tinned peaches, beef, corn, peas, and beans, into it. He told her to roll two blankets for him and tie them at both ends, which she did. Then he was ready to go.

She said, 'Take the gun, Pete.'

He shook his head at her. 'Listen now, Sarah; I'll have to parallel the trail John and Walter King will be using. That will be the only danger, and as long as John is being careful, we won't meet.'

'Make a noise,' said Sarah.

Pete would do that, of course. Also though, he explained which route he would use. He wanted her to know exactly where he would be. Not that he expected to be in any trouble, himself, but if he were needed, or if something arose he should know about, at least Sarah would be aware of how to locate him.

He kissed her cheek and left the store. She stood in a window watching him cross to the Land Rover, climb in when one of the strangers opened a rear door, then the car turned in the middle of the road and went off northward.

There were three elements of danger. One involved an accidental meeting with John and Walter King on the trail.

The second danger had to do with the strangers catching Pete slipping away from them in the night. The third peril would only arise if either of the large men began to suspect anything.

Pete promised himself to negate the third danger, and with only a little bit of luck to also avoid the other two. He was confident, as they bounced along the rutted road as far as the spongy hump where the oldtime fort had once stood, and there left the car, took up their light packs and started walking.

For a mile he kept to a westerly course. It was still bright enough so that the strangers, if they had compasses, would have detected any drift one way or another. But when they got into the forest the shadows darkened everything, and here, by keeping the men moving, by constantly twisting this way and that to avoid trees, deadfalls, patches of spiked underbrush, it was possible to drop southward until he was sure they were well beyond the usual trail, the one John and Walter King would certainly use.

Mid-way through the second mile one of the men hooked his foot under a root and fell heavily. Pete was sure the ankle had been sprained, but the man only cursed for a few moments, until the worst of the wrenching pain was past, then let his partner help him to his feet.

'Take five,' said the uninjured man to Pete. 'We need a little rest anyway.'

There was a creek close by. Pete took them to it, found a mossy place for the man who had fallen, broke out some tinned peaches and handed each man a can. For himself, there was tinned beef which he liked either hot or cold. He did not like tinned peaches; in fact Pete Sancroix did not like anything that was very sweet.

The blue-eyed man carved off the lids of the tins with a wicked-bladed hunting knife, handed one to his friend, and began eating peach-halves off the end of his big knife. He grinned at Pete.

'When I was a kid we used to go out like this, but its been a long time.'

Pete nodded. 'In upstate Massachusetts,' he murmured, confirming what the blue-eyed man had said. After all, he had said they were from Boston.

The stranger answered right back, making a correction. 'In New York,' he exclaimed, then suddenly caught himself.

Pete went right on eating his bully-beef as though he hadn't heard the correction, and hadn't afterwards seen the look on the blue-eyed man's face.

The interlude passed easily, as Pete had felt that it would if he let it. After all, these men were seeking Walter King, and perhaps even John Carbeau. They were *not* worrying about the storekeeper, Peter Sancroix — fortunately.

The tan-eyed man flexed his twisted ankle. It was sore, he confessed, but otherwise it would be fit enough with movement and exercise. He swore with disgust over his mishap until both Pete and the other large man assured him those things could happen at any moment to anyone.

He did, though, wonder how much farther they would be travelling before bedding down for the night. Pete shrugged. 'A mile; it will be dark after that. But we can camp right here if you wish. In the morning the ankle might be better.'

The tan-eyed man said, 'If I don't use it tonight, by morning it'll be swollen twice the size of my foot.' He stood up and said, 'Let's go.'

Any other time Pete might have admired the man's stamina. Now, he resumed the lead by directing the strangers over the roughest parts of the terrain. Within an hour the tan-eyed man was ready to rest again. It was still light out, but in the heart of the ancient forest the gloom was general and deep. Occasionally shafts of filtered light struck through. Where Pete halted the second time beside another creek, this one narrow and not deep enough to flow very much longer, the tan-eyed man sat to unlace his boot. Afterwards he massaged the sore ankle. But when Pete was solicitous, the man said, 'Hell, if I'd been looking where I was going it wouldn't have happened,' and grinned. He was tough, Pete decided, and rough, and in his own element he would also be self-sufficient. Of course what that added up to was a dangerous adversary.

Pete didn't worry. This was *his* element, perhaps not as much as it was Carbeau's element, or McLaughlin's, or most of the other indigenous people, but at least for now, and in his present company, it was Pete's element and he was master.

He made a tiny fire, cooked the evening meal, and although none of them were very hungry, they sat as men will do, with backs to trees, their bodies relaxed, and talked while toying with their food.

The strangers knew lots of jokes, and were affable men. The only time they seemed intent was when they started asking questions about old Jacques McLaughlin.

Pete told them the truth; old Jacques was a widower, a lifelong trapper, a gaunt, sinewy, tough and resourceful man who knew Portage Valley and the mountains in all directions probably better than anyone else alive.

The blue-eyed man caught Pete's attention. 'Is he, by any chance, related to John Carbeau?'

Pete blinked in spite of himself. It startled him, but after reflecting upon it a moment or two he had to conclude that it shouldn't have surprised him. If he had been in the stranger's boots he'd have wondered too. After all, they knew John was Josephine's father, and they also knew — now — where Walter King was. Putting it all together made the question reasonable.

'No relation,' replied Pete. 'Well, I've never heard either of them say that they were related.' He smiled. 'Maybe, if a person went back far enough it would turn up that they are. All Cree seemed to be related.'

The blue-eyed man wasn't to be diverted. 'And as you said before, if a stranger shows up everyone knows about it.'

'Yes.' Pete thought he knew what was coming.

'But how is it, then, that this stranger spent the winter with McLaughlin and no one knew about it until this spring?'

Pete smiled broadly. 'Wait. By the time we reach the cabin you'll understand what kind of a trip it would be in wintertime. A whole army could camp out there, and no one would find them until spring or summer.'

They finished eating. The blue-eyed man had more cigars, but neither Pete nor the other man accepted, so the blue-eyed man smoked by himself. He was comfortable. So was his companion, whose ankle, though a little swollen, seemed not to be hurting much, nor very seriously wrenched. Pete thought it was too bad; he also thought the tan-eyed man had a fairly extensive knowledge of sprains and wrenches. He was curious about his companions, but had no difficulty subjugating it. Maybe he would learn more and maybe he would not; what he was primarily interested in was getting away from them.

He no longer felt confident of losing them in the forest. He had seen neither of them with a compass in hand, but he had a feeling that, compass or not, they would be capable of back-tracking.

Of course, the longer he dwelt upon the capabilities of those two men, the more it was borne in upon him that he was probably in just as much danger as was Walter King. Perhaps more danger because it was highly unlikely the strangers would see anything very funny about being abandoned in the forest.

Well, he was committed, and as he told himself when he twisted around to spread his blankets, he was not exactly a babe-in-arms himself.

The blue-eyed man finished his smoke, stubbed out the cigar, asked his friend how the ankle felt, and when he was assured the ankle was better than expected, the blue-eyed man lay back without another word, composing himself for sleep.

It took a little longer for the other man to bed down, but Pete was in no hurry. He didn't intend to slip away until he was certain it was perfectly safe to do so, and meanwhile he was fed, comfortable, and resting.

There were owls calling back and forth, and once a wolf sang out. Otherwise, excepting the gurgle of creek-water, Pete could lie there ostensibly watching the high tangle of tree-limbs, while actually keeping an eye on his companions.

It took the man with the sore ankle longer to get to sleep. At first he seemed disposed to talk, but Pete scotched that by tipping up onto his side looking away from the man, and even afterwards when he rolled the other way so he could see them both, he gave a creditable imitation of a very tired man.

He thought it had to be about eleven o'clock when both of the strangers were sprawled in slumber. For an hour Pete had been alternating between concentrating on the breathing of those men, and the sounds roundabout amidst the trees.

Finally, he rolled off the blankets, rolled across pine needles to the very edge of the little creek, then sat up. His companions were as limp as rag dolls. Pete got to his feet, glided clear of the campsite, moved deeper among the trees, and within three minutes was gone.

He went north as far as the trail he'd used earlier getting out to McLaughlin's cabin, but this time he struck out back towards McLean, and he jogged. Not constantly, he wasn't in that good a physical condition, but he had the whole night ahead of him, and he was confident of reaching the village in plenty of time, so speed was less important than persistence.

It was past midnight when he came to the site of the old fort. The Land Rover was sitting there in soft moonlight. He went right on past it, jogging again, and reached the outskirts of the village.

A few lights still burned, but nine-tenths of the buildings, cabins and stores both, were dark and silent. He slowed, finally, when he saw the lamp turned low in his own parlour. He turned in at the gate, got to the front porch, and paused a moment to look all around. He didn't expect to see anyone, and he was not surprised in this respect. He reached for the knob and turned it.

Sarah was sitting in a chair near the fireplace, sound asleep. When he awakened her she said she had gone to Josephine after closing the store for the day, to explain what Pete was doing. She then wanted to know where Pete had left the strangers, and when he told her, Sarah got to her feet and went back to the door with him saying she would go with him to the Carbeau place.

He mumbled a little, not in favour of this, but it wasn't anything very critical so there was no argument. Later, at the Carbeau's kitchen door, around back, John recognized her before he recognized Pete, and drew them both inside a lighted, warm kitchen.

John pointed towards the moon-lighted parlour. Josephine was in there, he said, with Walter. Then John smiled and nodded his head at Pete.

'Sarah told Josie what you were doing. It was a good thing.'

Sancroix grimaced. 'Maybe those men won't think so in the morning.' He went to the stove and hefted the coffee pot. John took the hint and went rummaging through cupboards for cups.

10

A Kitchen Council

When Josephine brought Walter King to the kitchen her cheeks were flushed and there was a quicksilver flash to her glance.

Of course she was anxious; she knew the danger and the risk perhaps as well as any of them, and after Pete Sancroix had related for her benefit and Walter's what he had been through since mid-afternoon, she knew even better, how long was the arm of a mean and unrelenting old man.

Her father got more cups and poured more coffee. For someone who had just been through a gruelling trek, John seemed in excellent spirits and un-tired. Sarah mentioned that and he smiled at her when he said, 'I am never conscious of getting old when I'm out in the valley. It's only when I come back to the village and see how many people are younger, that I feel that I must be getting tired pretty soon now because I'm an old man.'

Pete grinned. He probably wouldn't have said it quite the same way but for a fact he felt far less tired this time after a long hike than he'd felt the other time.

He mentioned the two strangers in that regard, but Walter contradicted him at once. 'They may be green, as green as I was when I first came up here, but don't sell them short on toughness.'

'Or resourcefulness,' put in Josephine. 'Mr King doesn't hire blunderers nor weaklings.'

Pete asked the question that bothered him most, of Walter King. 'You don't have to put up with this. How is it that you do?'

Walter, still wearing his curly, light beard, leaned against the wall, coffee cup in hand, and gently smiled at

Sancroix. 'It will be easier all around if I simply manage to keep out of my grandfather's control for another month.'

Pete nodded. 'That can be arranged. We have law up here too, you know. It is a fairly simple matter to get a constable to — .'

'The point is,' said Walter, not waiting for Pete to finish, 'if I can stay out of their way without notoriety it will be so much better. I realize how it looks to you — as though I'm the intended victim of an abduction.'

'Well,' demanded Pete loudly, 'aren't you?'

Walter gazed over the heads of the older people to Josephine, and she smiled softly at him, then dropped her gaze to Sancroix as she said, 'Uncle Pete, even if those men you left in the forest managed to find Walter, and if they persuaded him to return to New York with them, he couldn't possibly say he'd been abducted.'

'Couldn't he?' exclaimed Pete,

shooting his brows straight up. 'What would he call it, then?'

'But think of what something like that would do, Uncle Pete. The newspapers would jump on it as the juiciest scandal of the year. It would injure his brother, his friends who own shares in the companies. It would depress all King Syndicate shares, and it would force old Mr King to fight back, and above everything else, we don't want that.'

Pete looked at his wife, at John Carbeau, then into his coffee cup. He had nothing more to say on the subject. He seemed far from convinced that Josephine's argument held any valid merit, but he was unwilling doggedly to press his point, so he sat glumly while Walter tried to explain a little more fully.

'Thousands of people own King Syndicate stocks, Mr Sancroix. The minute a scandal hit the newspapers those people would stand to lose an awful lot of money. Moreover, a scandal would also hurt the company. I talked this over with my brother Sanford. He tried to dissuade me from even marrying until after Grandfather King dies. But that was two years ago when I first fell in love, and all that has happened since is that Grandfather King has got older and tougher.'

'And meaner, evidently,' muttered John. 'Anyone wish more coffee?'

No one did.

Josephine crossed to Walter's side and for a moment Sarah's dark glance softened. Then she firmed up again and said, 'Well, what are we to do now? Walter, you can't stay here. And Pete, if you don't return to those men in the forest they will know you are also mixed up in all this.'

Pete wasn't too concerned. With a heavy shrug he growled his response. 'Let them. I'll tell you what I think: Grandfather King may hold his world in the palm of his hand, but *we* up here also hold *our* world in the palms of *our* hands too. Let those men find their way back out of the forest tomorrow.

By then we should be agreed that we tell them nothing, help them in no way, and if we must, why then I think we can organize the whole village against them. Let Grandfather King find a way around *that* kind of opposition.'

Walter smiled at old Pete. 'It was wishful thinking on my part of course, since I'm only a visitor up here, but out at the cabin I had an idea that perhaps something like that might be a better answer than if I fled.' He groped for Josephine's hand at his side and gripped it. 'But of course we're only talking like this because it sounds brave. Mr Sancroix, you don't know my grandfather.'

'Hah!' snorted Pete. 'And your grandfather doesn't know us, Walter.'

'Mr Sancroix, it's quixotic but not very sensible.'

Sarah nodded without much enthusiasm. 'He's right,' she told her husband. 'Think about it a moment, Pete. That old man has more than enough money to buy this whole village.'

'And if you all get involved,' said Walter, 'you'll only be borrowing someone else's trouble. I couldn't stand for that, even though you did it voluntarily.'

John, sitting relaxed with his soft gaze upon his daughter, said, 'Well, Sarah, how could that old man buy what's not for sale? At my age money means very little. Even if I could buy your store, it wouldn't be the same when I went there next winter to sit by the stove and watch the snow come down. You see? Two hundred and fifty million dollars isn't worth that one pleasure to me. So how could this old man buy me?'

'Not you,' replied Sarah. 'But he could buy others around here.'

'What good would that do?' asked old John. 'He couldn't buy Jacques or Pete or me, or you or Josie. What good would it do for him to buy everyone else in the village, even if he could?'

John slowly wagged his head. 'It takes time to stalk a moose or to fight a war, Sarah. All we need is one month.' John and Pete exchanged a look. 'I haven't known very many people in my lifetime,' exclaimed John, 'who would sell their self-respect. I don't even think he could buy very many of the people in McLean, Sarah. We've never had much; probably we never will have much. But by now, for most of us, we don't want much.'

Walter and Josephine, listening to this exchange, both started to speak, interrupting one another. Josephine smiled at Walter and checked herself so he could be heard.

'Look; those are beautiful sentiments, Mr Carbeau, but I still can't allow it. I'll find another hiding-place. As you said, it's only for a month.'

'Where?' demanded Sarah, always the realist.

Walter hesitated, then said, 'Somewhere. I don't know, but if I get enough of a head-start tonight, I'll find a place.' He tightened his hold on Josephine's hand, which the older people saw.

Pete Sancroix raised his eyes to his wife's face. 'We're already involved. Do you see what time it is? I couldn't get back to those men before dawn. They'll know anyway before — '

A heavy hand falling across the front door boomed through the cabin, stopping Pete's words in mid-breath, and nearly stopping the hearts of all those people in the kitchen. The knocking was repeated. For several seconds no one moved, but Josephine finally stirred, turned as though to go out through the house to the front door, but Walter held her back by the hand.

John rose, pushed back his chair and shooting an apprehensive look at the others, left the kitchen. At once Sarah came to life. 'They can't come in here without John's permission. Pete, take Walter out the back way and down to our place.'

Josephine held up a hand for silence. Voices came back as far as the kitchen from the front of the house. Masculine voices, deep and strong, but indistinguishable. Pete, leaning to listen, uttered a quick, hard little curse and sprang up.

'Jacques,' he said.

He was correct. It was McLaughlin. John brought the tall, lean old man out into the kitchen where McLaughlin blinked briefly in the light, then gave each one of them a hard look, finally settling his steady dark stare upon Pete.

'They are coming back,' he said, without bothering to explain either who 'they' were or how he knew, both of which were not as important as his words. 'When I found them they were looking for a trail. I thought at first they were simply lost campers and showed them the way to McLean. Then they mentioned you, and I knew. One limps badly so they won't be here for a long time — maybe two hours or more — but when I got away from them to hurry ahead, they were mad.'

Pete threw up his hands as he looked around. 'Well, there you are,' he exclaimed. 'Now how can you say we aren't involved.'

'I'll leave at once,' exclaimed Walter, and old Jacques slowly shook his head. 'They are expecting that. I think these men are better trackers in their own environment than any of us would be at eluding them. Walt, if you leave the valley they'll run you down without very much trouble.'

For once Sarah agreed with a view different from the one she'd been espousing. 'Jacques is right, Walter.' She looked at McLaughlin. 'Can you hide him, Jacques?'

The old recluse nodded his head without any hesitation. 'In any one of a hundred places.'

Walter had doubts. 'They'll hire a native to track me down.'

Jacques and John Carbeau thinly smiled. Even Pete Sancroix, although he did not smile, had something to say to contradict that. 'My boy, if Jacques McLaughlin doesn't want you to be found, except for John here, I don't know anyone on this earth who could find you in Portage Valley.'

Carbeau chuckled and winked at old Jacques. 'I couldn't. He knows the country better than I do.'

Josephine was beginning to regain some of the colour she had lost when that thumping great roll of knuckles had struck across the front door.

Sarah too, looked, if not exactly relieved, at least encouraged. She was never quite enthusiastic about anything. Now, her hard-headedness prompted her to ask Jacques if he realized that he would be making dangerous enemies, and he nodded his answer at her without saying anything for a moment.

'What can this rich old American do to me, up there at my cabin?'

It was a simple question, but a sound one. Jacques looked over at Walter and winked, a display of human feeling the others in the room had not seen him display in many, many years. Not since his wife had died.

'You see Walt and I put in a long winter. I told him all the old Cree legends, and even taught him some of the language, and that makes us related. A man can't do anything better than protect his own, can he?'

Pete Sancroix's dark, strong gaze brightened with appreciation. Jacques had just put into words Pete's own lifelong feelings — only in reverse. Pete had always considered the Crees *his* family, and now here was the old Cree, Jacques McLaughlin, expressing the same feelings towards fair and blue-eyed Walter King.

'Then,' said John Carbeau, 'you had better leave, Jacques.'

But McLaughlin shrugged that off and went to get himself a cup of black coffee. Over one broad, bony shoulder he said, 'There is time yet. I'll rest here for a while. It was a long trek today.' He looked at Walter, at

Josephine, sniffed the hot coffee and wrinkled his nose before lowering the cup. 'Go outside,' he said, 'and look at the moon. I'll come for you, Walt, when it's time to go.'

Jacques McLaughlin evidently hadn't lost as much human feeling as people had thought he might have, over the years. Or perhaps that hunter's moon had reminded him of other times, long gone now, almost lost in the mists of memory, when he too had taken a beautiful Cree girl out to see the warm summer night.

11

A Long Night

To make an inland country wet and flourishing during the hot months there must be long, snowy winters, otherwise snow-cover melts, watersheds run brimful for a short time, and underground water-levels drop and drop, until roots are no longer nourished. Then the land turns dry and hot and usually brown.

The summers around McLean were never very long; four months in the good years, otherwise frost might resume its visit in early September. But this past winter it had been cold a long time, the snow-cover was still very deep in the high mountains, creeks and lakes were full, and even though mid-July had come and gone and every day after that, like most of the nights, was either downright hot, or blessedly warm, there was reason to believe the summer would linger almost until the first of October this year.

'You see that moon,' explained Josephine, 'the way it is dusty looking? Well, that is the sure sign. Ask anyone around McLean. We'll have leaves turning red and gold but there won't be any really bad weather until after the first of October. Maybe not even until November.'

Walter gazed at the moon as they moved slowly across the rear garden of her father's home where the view was unobstructed, and later when he dropped his eyes to her lifted face he smiled.

'It is the old hunter's moon,' he said, keeping the smile. 'Now is the time for the men to go off in bands to the high country for bear and moose and deer and caribou, and to the lakes for fish to be smoked and made into pemmican.'

She laughed. 'A winter with old

Jacques McLaughlin, and you'll never be the same again.'

His eyes twinkled. 'As a matter of fact I *do* feel an urge to go bring in the meat.'

'Well, my love, I can tell you in advance that I *don't* have any desire to sit by a smoky old fire and cut it into strips to smoke and dry. I prefer the supermarkets.'

'You're a disgrace to the Cree,' he intoned, and she rippled the night with her laughter again.

'Isn't it the truth?'

Near a patch of dark earth there were squash vines, potato creepers spreading toward some conical sticks leaning, and tied at the top, where pole-beans were climbing upwards.

She pointed to some sturdy plants with red stalks and coarse, large green leaves. 'Rhubarb. When I was little my father and I would stand out here and eat it raw.' She laughed. 'It was terrible.'

'Then why did you eat it?'

She took his arm and held it close as she leaned closer. 'My father made the sun rise, the moon set, the snow fall, and the rhubarb grow.'

He slid an arm round her waist. 'You are a lot luckier than I was, as a child. Maybe that's what shaped me the way I am. It's not that I can't adjust to the business world, or that I'm rebelling, as my grandfather keeps claiming. It's that I'm just a misfit in his financial world. I like wealth — I'm not a pure nut — but it's just not everything.' He squeezed her. 'I wouldn't ever want a kid of mine to grow up wondering when his parents might return from Europe so he could see if they really are as he remembers them.'

They had been through this before, so she understood. What she failed to understand was how his grandfather — old men were supposed to mellow, to learn wisdom — should be so adamantly opposed to the things Walter felt. Once, regardless of how long ago, he too had known love and warmth.

He'd married, had raised a child.

She looked up at the dusty old moon again. 'Do you know that if we had never met, nothing would be changed, Walt?'

He didn't fathom her meaning and turned her so he could see down into her dark eyes. She said, 'It would have been someone else, Walt, somewhere else. Your grandfather is very strong. Strong men touch all the lives around them. That's why I've never just given up; because if it wasn't me, he would still find something else you wanted opposite to what he wants for you.'

'Pretty involved,' he muttered, and started to move a little closer to the garden patch. A snow-owl startled them by suddenly rising from the ground like an explosion of white feathers, in among the corn rows. It shot upwards with a frantic and noisy beating of wings. Evidently it had been hunting, had found a mouse or other small rodent among the corn rows, and had swooped down for the kill. The arrival of the people had frightened it.

When they recovered from their astonishment he said, 'The spirit of a shaman,' and grinned.

Her response was the same little smile she'd shown before. 'I don't think I'll let you go back out to Jacques's cabin. You're going to end up worshipping water-sprites and cloud-spirits.'

They moved leisurely along the front of the garden old John planted every spring, had in fact planted in that same place for as far back as his daughter could remember.

The night was warm and full of fragrance. It was velvety and quiet. The hour was late, and doubtless that accounted for much of what was serene, but also this was not a part of the world where people had reason to fear sleep or fear rest. Even the animals led a leisurely existence.

'I think,' he told her, 'we'll buy a piece of land up here, and build a snug cabin. And every summer we can come back.'

She liked that. 'But you can't paint it. And when you come up in the summertime you can't wear a tie or change your shirt too often.'

He stopped. 'Do you like it here? I mean, do you *really* like it up here, Josie?'

She turned cautious. 'I like it. I'd have to, wouldn't I? This is where I grew up, where my parents lived, where all my relations live — or are buried. But I wouldn't ever want to come back to live year-round, if that's what you had in mind.'

'No. Not year-round. But Josie, old Jacques and I hiked to lakes where there wasn't a single man-track on the snow. We saw beaver playing and otter making slides in the mud. There was nothing between us and God but solitude. I want our kids to see that, to *feel* it, at least to know there is that other world. Not necessarily to become part of it, but at least to know it.'

She reached up with both hands to draw his face down and kiss him. Then she lowered her hold to his waist and clung close.

They were standing like that when a low whistle made them break apart and turn. Jacques was over by the corner of the cabin, recognizable by his height and thinness. She gave one convulsive hug, then turned with Walt to cross the intervening distance, and she was silent now, still and silent and fatalistic. If anyone had been out there to notice it, they might have seen a similarity between her way of accepting things, and Sarah Sancroix's same philosophical fatalism.

Jacuqes had two bundles. He handed one to Walter, then he looked at Josephine rather thoughtfully. 'Your father will know where he is, and it won't be so far that if you can't wait, you can walk over there.'

She smiled and moved in to kiss the old man's dark and leathery cheek. He didn't change expression at all, but he

147

touched her lightly with a hand.

'Don't worry. A month isn't very long. When that moon returns looking the same way, it will have passed — a whole month.'

Jacques turned and found something very interesting in the rough planking at his back. Josephine went into her lover's arms and hung there as closely as she could press, then they kissed and he stepped away, moving past so that Jacques saw him. The older man didn't look back.

Josephine followed at a distance until they grew dim in tree-shadows crossing the yard towards open country northward. When she heard a sound and looked, Sarah was there, tall and handsome in the moonlight, and as patient as she had been brought up to be.

'It's late, child, and your father is going to bed now. My man is walking home, and I want to catch up with him. You should go inside now.'

Josephine didn't let the older woman

see her face. 'They went north,' she said simply.

'Well, those grandfather-men will be coming in from the west. Anyway, that's where Jacques said he will make their camp.'

Josephine finally turned. 'Is he going to stay with Walter?'

Sarah nodded.

Josie smiled a little and took the older woman's nearest hand and hung on to it 'People are good, Aunt Sarah.'

The answer she got to that was a little dry. 'Some of them are more good than others. But I guess you are right. Even Grandfather King, I suppose.' Sarah had to pause over that, struggling against her own hint of flintiness before also saying, 'Well, I guess it's just that we don't all know what good really is. What is good for you and Walter isn't good for Grandfather King.'

Sarah laid a hand upon the girl's shoulder, leaned and lightly kissed Josie, then freed her held-hand and turned. 'Go inside now, and lock the doors. Good-night, Josie.'

When she was alone again, Josephine leaned upon an old fence-post in front of the house and let the warm wash of moonlight cover her in its soft-pale magic. Love was nothing very new to her, not after so many months of having it fill her heart and motivate her thoughts, her dreams, her entire spirit. But she did not think, standing there now and dwelling upon it, that if she lived to be a hundred years old, she would ever be able to define it.

She also wondered — for the hundredth time — how it would have been between them if Walter's grandfather hadn't practically taken up arms against the marriage.

It wasn't *her*, she knew that, and the old man had even made it plain that who she was or what she was had nothing to do with it. He did not want Walter to marry. Even Walter's own father, dead now for many years, had entertained thoughts like that. Evidently the dead father had inherited more than just physical characteristics from the old man. At least to a point.

But it was late, and now that she was alone and the immediate crisis was past, she began to feel tired. She told herself once more that it did not matter how things *might* have been, because that was not how they *were*. Like Sarah, she was at heart at least in part, a realist. Most Crees were.

She turned, saw the soft moonlit outline of the old cabin, and felt an urge to cry, not out of sadness, not even out of a sense of relief that so far everything was working out; in fact she didn't cry, but she wanted to. And she didn't really know why.

She went around to the back of the house and entered the dark, warm kitchen with its coffee-fragrance, passed through the other rooms to her own place, and stood for a moment longer at a window gazing northward down the pale night. Then, finally, she began to get ready for bed.

It was past two o'clock in the morning.

12

Love is Triumph

Pete Sancroix was certainly entitled to his misgivings, and it would have helped if the two strangers had come stamping into the store soon after he opened the place for business, because at least then he was alone and braced for the meeting.

But they didn't arrive until almost eleven o'clock. By then John was at his usual place over by the cold stove, and there were customers moving among the counters.

Sarah was there, waiting on the trade. Jacques McLaughlin was also there, smoking a cigar with the blissful appreciation of a man who allowed himself such a luxury only very rarely. He was leaning on the wall over where the racks of rifles and shotguns made a dark background.

Not far from where Jacques stood was a clutter of steel traps suspended from a wooden dowel in the wall, and even closer was the pile of splendid Hudson's Bay blankets that no one would even look at now until the snow returned.

It took a good deal more money to maintain the inventory than most people realized. Actually, if Pete and Sarah had ever sat down and figured it out, they had more cash tied up in their inventory than their meagre monthly profit deserved.

But they had never figured that this was their reason for operating their store; they hadn't actually ever reasoned *what* that purpose was, except to make a living, and this morning, like just about every other morning, they served customers. But they also shot an occasional look towards the front door.

The two large men entered the emporium through that opening at a few minutes before eleven o'clock, one limping a little, and both of them freshly shaved and freshly dressed in clean clothing.

Pete, near his cash-drawer, saw them at once, and they saw him. They also saw John Carbeau, but the one person who seemed to hold their attention longest was Jacques McLaughlin, still nursing his cigar.

Pete leaned on the counter, slowly inclined his head, and said, 'Well, now you see how it is.'

The blue-eyed man was slow in replying. He crossed to the counter, studied Pete a moment, then shoved fisted hands into trouser pockets as he answered. 'We see. I wonder if *you* see how it is, Mr Sancroix? You jumped into a private matter with both feet last night. Except for you we'd have had Walt King.'

Old Jacques removed his cigar-stub. 'No you wouldn't have,' he said.

The blue-eyed man turned. 'You too, oldtimer? Why don't you just stay out of it? You did us a good turn last night. Let it stay like that.'

'Can't,' stated Jacques. 'We'd have met sooner or later anyway.'

The blue-eyed man looked mild as he said, 'Why? Because you may be related to the girl, or her father, or Sancroix here?'

'No. Because you were on your way to see me. My name is Jacques McLaughlin.'

Both the strangers looked in surprise at old Jacques, who resumed his puffing on the cigar. He had surprised them, palpably, and now seemed pleased to have done that. But he had no more to say.

The blue-eyed man looked at his companion, who went over to lean upon the counter so that he could shift some weight off the sprained ankle.

John finally spoke from his tilted-back chair over by the stove. 'Go back,' he said to the outlanders. 'You made an honest effort; it wasn't your fault that it failed. Now go back and tell that old man in New York you don't know where his grandson is, because it's the truth.'

The blue-eyed one sighed. 'I wish it was that easy,' he murmured, gazing steadily at Carbeau. 'But it isn't. We'll find Walter King, and we won't leave here until we do.'

Jacques smiled but no one else did. Pete looked over where his wife was watching and listening after getting rid of her last customer. Except for the two strangers and those involved with them, there were no other people in the store at the moment. It was getting along towards mid-day, the heat was becoming oppressive, and soon everyone would go home to eat. After lunchtime business might pick up again, although that was debatable since people tried to avoid going out in hot weather if they could.

'Look,' said the tan-eyed man, speaking for the first time. 'What is it to you people, anyway? Suppose my friend and I lay one thousand dollars on this counter, then walk out of here and do not return until the morning. However you divide it would be your business. All we'd ask would be that you produce young King. That's all. And in case you think we're here to harm him, believe me, folks, you can't imagine how wrong that is. Why, when we take him back home, he'll have more money to do with as he pleases than you people could even count.'

Pete looked at the others. They were silent from listening but not a single change had come to their defiant faces. He said, 'You had better make it more like a hundred thousand dollars.'

The tan-eyed man glared. 'Listen, Sancroix, if we tell Old Man King what you people did up here, and what you're trying to do now, he'd buy this place and burn it to the ground.'

'How would he buy what no one would sell him?'

'He'd buy the mortgages, the loans!'

Sarah gave a soft little laugh. 'There are no mortgages. We build our own

158

homes. No bank lends money up here. We're too far from Quebec and Montreal. Loans? You find them.'

The blue-eyed man fished out a cigar, lit it and shook his head. 'We don't want trouble,' he exclaimed, sounding slightly exasperated. 'Walter King won't be harmed. He won't be hurt in any way. Look; any two of you can return to New York with us and see for yourselves. Listen to me; my partner and I were simply hired to do a job. That's all. The same as you people have jobs to do. There's nothing wrong with — .'

'You waste a lot of words,' muttered old Jacques, looking with regret at the tiny, frayed stub of his cigar. 'You convince Walter that he ought to go with you, and no one here will lift a hand to keep it from happening.'

'How the hell do we convince him,' snapped the man with the sore ankle, 'if we can't find him to talk to him?'

'Tell me,' said old Jacques. 'I'll tell him.'

Both the large men stared at Jacques. For them, obviously, this was the first decent break so far. That stringly old tall, leathery man knew where Walter was. But if they had some comment to make about that, Jacques cut in before they could speak it.

Looking sombrely at them he said, 'I am over seventy. This is my country, my way of life. You can't even walk through a mile of forest without hurting yourselves. If you want to try trailing or tracking me, I won't stop you. But you'll never find Walter — and you *might* find something more than a twisted ankle.'

'A threat?' asked the large, blue-eyed man.

Jacques shook his head. 'No. I never make threats. Besides, I don't know you so I can't dislike you, can I? You aren't in New York City now, that's all. Here, you are fishes out of water.' Jacques nodded towards the tan-eyed man's swollen ankle. 'What I meant was that a sprained ankle is

160

nothing compared to muskeg-sand or snake bite.'

The blue-eyed man smoked for a moment, still making his rather chilly study of old Jacques, then he dropped his gaze to John, over by the stove. 'Mr Carbeau, could we speak to your daughter?'

John nodded and started to speak, but Sarah's sharp retort cut through first. 'What for? You and that old devil you work for have caused enough grief already. You want to try and bribe her too. No; you can't see her!'

The blue-eyed man twisted towards Pete. 'Is she your wife?' he asked, and when Sancroix nodded the big man's gaze got sardonic. 'What I'm trying my level best to do, Mr Sancroix, is get this thing resolved without a lot of unnecessary hard feelings. We would just like to talk to everyone who is involved. That's all. Make a good effort to make folks listen to reason.'

John said, 'Let me speak to my daughter first. If she will see you, I'll bring her to the store in the morning. Is that all right?'

For the first time the blue-eyed man relaxed and almost smiled. 'That'll be fine, Mr Carbeau. We'll appreciate it.'

John did not relax nor change mood, not even in the face of this obvious thawing on the part of the opposition. 'I don't think you could change my daughter's mind in a thousand years, though. Women are never very reasonable, not when they are at their best, but when they are in love . . .' John suddenly felt black eyes boring into him and looked over to find Sarah Sancroix darkly staring. He said, 'Well, *young* women, I'm talking about,' and if that only made everything worse he didn't seem to know it.

None of the other men were very sensitive to Sarah's presence either. While there was a little lull, Jacques left the dark part of the store where he had been standing, marched across in front of everyone and went out of the front door into the golden, hot sunlight.

The tan-eyed man looked after him, with an obvious thought, but did not move. Then Jacques turned and strolled southward out of sight.

The blue-eyed man straightened up off the counter with a little smile. 'Well, we've made some progress,' he said, and raised a hand to his hat in Sarah's direction, then went out of the store followed by his limping friend.

John smiled and Pete's dark eyes twinkled. Only Sarah didn't seem pleased or mollified. She pointed a finger at John and said, 'You shouldn't make Josephine come here and listen to those men. She's had a year and more of trouble as it is, from people like that. You should have told them . . . '

'Yes, Sarah?'

'Well. You should have told them to go where Pete says people should go who don't pay their bills on time!'

The men laughed, and that sound echoing round the huge old log store-building, marked the end of the uncomfortable confrontation, at least for the time being.

'The blue-eyed one will follow Jacques,' said John, leaving his chair to go and peer out of the window, southward.

'He may need the exercise,' stated Pete, and opened the cash drawer to remove a slip of paper and make a notation upon it. When John moved to the doorway and started through, Pete called after him. 'Where are you going?'

'Home,' replied John calmly. 'It's a fine day for visiting with my daughter.'

The afternoon came, and wore along, and more vacationers arrived, some pulling caravans behind protesting cars. A few were noisy and complaining, but generally such people were too intrigued at finding themselves in an old Indian town to do more than walk the sidewalks staring in windows, staring at the natives, or whispering back and forth.

Caroline Laughlin had once said the best way in the world for McLean to really bring holidayers flocking in would be to send away to one of those mail-order houses down in the States that specialized in selling costumes, outfit everyone with Indian pants and shirts, even those feathered bonnets it was alleged that all Indians wore, and make McLean *look* like an Indian village.

That suggestion had caused roars of laughter and hoots of derision to rise up all over town, but there was some merit to the idea. Even Sarah agreed there was, although she also said, being very practical, they would have to get some books somewhere and learn how Indians acted, otherwise the whole thing would look fake.

Nothing had ever been done.

People came to the general store, though, and confidentially asked Pete if the natives were annoyed by having holidayers clutter up their country, and Pete's unfailing response was to tell them in low-voiced confidence that as long as they always remembered to raise their right hand, palm outward whenever meeting an Indian in the forest or out in the valley, and say 'How' very loudly, they would always be welcome.

Sarah was furious once when she was out with friends gathering blueberries, and a plump Jewish lady from New York's Bronx had risen from beyond a clump of bushes and had said, 'How!'

After that Pete was careful.

Still, when people began drifting into the store to stand and stare at racks of weapons, mounds of steel traps, and also at Pete and Sarah, that day after the meeting with Mr King's men, Pete went over and told his wife he had to go up and get a bottle of beer or he was going to say something insulting to the next person who asked him if he was an Indian.

Sarah, who neither drank nor approved of it in her man, frowned down her nose. Then patted his hand. She did not condone what he was going to do, at least not out loud, but neither did she argue against it.

After Pete had stamped out of the building heading towards that café across the road where he'd hailed those two strangers the afternoon before, Sarah stood and stoically regarded the staring, silent holidayers, wondering when, and if, they would buy anything, quite unaware that her tall stance and entirely expressionless face was exactly the reason none of them ever did buy anything — they didn't dare.

But Sarah didn't really care; she was thinking of something else anyway. She was as sure as she was alive, that love was going to triumph for Josie and her young man.

13

A Tryst

Caroline Laughlin, village busybody and gossip, came by to ask Josephine Carbeau if she wouldn't like to join Caroline and two other middle-aged women, and go to pick blueberries beyond town over near a spit of forest where Caroline had a special place.

John thought it was an excellent idea. He even went searching in a shed for the buckets, and turned up an old pair of leather gloves. No one could actually pick blueberries wearing heavy gloves because the berries were both small and tender, but in mid-summer it was always prudent to have a pair of gloves along, not just to push past thorns and nettles, but also to first make certain, before removing the gloves, one was not going to plunge a hand in where bees and yellow-jackets might be lurking.

Josephine hesitated. She would rather have stayed at home. John urged her to take the gloves and buckets and go. She wasn't doing anyone any good sitting around the house wearing a long face, he said.

He had already explained about the visit of the strangers to the store, of the discussion down there, and of the suggestion that she meet the strangers down there the following morning.

Her reaction had been one of both dissent and indignation. After she'd denounced the strangers John had said, 'Listen to me; you have a month to go, and every day you can make those men waste is one more day in your favour. So tomorrow we'll go to the store and talk, but today you go gather berries. Maybe one of those men will be watching. If so, you see, we will make them waste another day.'

It was true, of course, but it seemed like a tedious way to triumph.

Josephine would much rather have had a confrontation; a conclusion one way or another.

She met Caroline and the other two women up at the north end of town, and when Josephine asked how far it was to the berry patch, Caroline winked and said it was only about a mile; that no one else knew of this spot because it was generally thought all the patches close-in had been cleaned out long ago.

There was a growth of brambles on both sides of the berry patch which made it unlikely anyone would even find it accidentally, at least for a while yet, and meanwhile Caroline and her friends wouldn't have to trek out across the valley for miles like almost everyone else had to do.

The other women, both Caroline's age, were both known to Josephine. One was a grandmother already, with a daughter and son-in-law who had moved over the line down to Minneapolis in the States. Because Josephine had attended school with this woman's daughter, the conversation between them was lively.

The other woman was the widow of a big, laughing man Josephine remembered quite well, who had been killed by the falling limb of a huge pine tree while working at a logging camp. This woman too, had children, but they had been quite a bit younger and although Josephine remembered them, she'd never had much in common with them.

It was warm. The farther they got from the village, and the nearer they got to the wet muskegs, the greater were the swarms of gnats and mosquitoes. Normally gnats were only a nuisance, but mosquitoes in the north country were not only extremely large, and always ravenous, but it always took the heat to bring them out.

Caroline and the other women had bottles of repellent. Otherwise, berry-gathering would have a been a genuine torment. Near the first swamp-like wet muskeg they stopped to smear the repellent over their faces, necks, and hands. Otherwise they were protected by clothing. The repellent worked. At least the mosquitoes did not bite but they persistently buzzed round the women, which was nearly as bad until one became accustomed to the harassment.

There were trails in all directions from the village, mostly re-made, except of course where they had been worn through living stone by, first, generations of moccasin-clad people, and later, by more generations of people wearing boots.

But the trails did not always lead anywhere. They occasionally ended upon a creek-bank, or faded out at a muskeg. Where they struck stone they were even less liable to detection unless it was a very old trail.

The one Caroline took hadn't been made by children; it deviated from true northeast only where it had to, at thistle patches, or where the ground underfoot became soggy, and once near an old trap-set where the ground had been dug out to a depth of perhaps a foot. Otherwise it headed directly for a low hillock of shale-stone, went up and over that knoll, and down the far side.

The women stopped on the low roll of land the way people always do, out of ancient urging, and swept the countryside all around with a look, before starting down the far side.

Behind them, to the southwest, lay the village, paintless, weathered, crowded in close although there was all the bare, open land in the world for it to spread out over, and for once without a single streamer of smoke rising from any of the tin stove-pipes.

Otherwise, farther off, stood the timeless mountains, the pine-spiked sidehills, and the vast lift and roll of valley floor, not flat but nearly so, in comparison to its restricting, surrounding slopes.

Green growth flourished everywhere. Even where it was rocky the soil was rich. No one knew how many different varieties of plant-life grew in Portage Valley; as yet no one had arrived to make the study.

And as far as Josephine could determine, there was no movement. She wasn't sure whether she'd expected to be followed or not. Her father hadn't mentioned it and neither had her companions of the berry-picking expedition. She was lulled by these things as well as by her own inclination to scoff at anything so melodramatic.

Caroline pointed to a great tangle of thistles and brambles down the far side of the slope and out where heat bouncing off the side of their low knoll kept things growing as though in a hot-house. They couldn't actually see the berries, which were small and more purple than blue, but to experienced pickers the shape of berry-bush leaves, and the particular shade of green, were as good.

Caroline explained that she'd been returning from a visit to one of the families living beyond McLean, northeast towards the areas people farmed, when she had accidentally discovered the hidden patch of berries.

The other women were pleased because not only were the berries plump and sweet, but also because they were plentiful. It was very unusual for a patch of berry bushes to be undetected this close to the village.

The women spread out, wading through brambles in their search for berries, gabbling like geese, occasionally saying something sharp and ringing where a thorn raked skin or tore cloth.

Josephine, quieter, less zealous about something the older women had done most of their lives and considered important, but which she had never done out of necessity, worked her way round to the north where it seemed the brambles were fewer and the stalks of thistles were more readily avoided because they grew tall instead of crawling over the ground.

The berries on that side of the patch were farther between, perhaps because the heat was minimal over there, but Josephine was in no hurry to fill her bucket.

It was rather pleasant, listening to the older women, feeling the heat, smelling that summer-scent, which was not actually a fragrance as much as it was the smell of fecund earth, damp and warm, mingling with the smell of growing things.

She paused twice to look around. That little low roll of land cut them off from sight of the village, so there was nothing man-made to be seen. It was like being alone in a new universe — except for the rosary-like recitation of names of children, relations and friends by the other women, making a steady trill of sound.

She smiled to herself as she listened. Caroline was an ambulatory history of everyone and everything connected with the village. She could tick off relationships and prove who was related to whom without any hesitation at all. She was also the living-breathing repository of everything titillating, salacious, or shameful, about her neighbours and endless relations, but one thing that Josephine finally noticed, and felt some surprise over, was that during the rapid flow of Caroline's most delightful gossipy tidbits, she never once mentioned the young man who had wintered with Jacques McLaughlin — who was Caroline's uncle several times removed — although that one bit of information fulfilled all the best requirements for a special category of gossip.

Josephine kept listening and waiting, but Caroline, over across the bushes and beyond Josie's sight, touched blithely upon everything except that one topic.

It occurred to Josephine that someone had remonstrated with Caroline. But knowing Caroline as she did, and had known her all her life, Josephine knew how absolutely independent and cantankerous the woman could be and usually was. The surest way to get Caroline to dwell upon a subject would be to suggest that she *not* dwell upon it.

Josephine halted in her picking for a bit and straightened up to rest her back. Sore backs and aching muscles were the occupational hazards of berry-picking. She raised a hand to brush back hair that had dropped low, and she turned once left, once right, to loosen tightened muscles. It was when she turned right that she saw him standing in front of a medium-sized, second-growth fir tree smiling at her, as still and motionless as though he had been carved of stone.

She checked an urge to call out, stooped to put her bucket down, then slowly made a complete circuit before facing him again. There was no one else in sight. That did not mean there was no one else *around*, which was what made her pick her way towards him looking very anxious.

He still hadn't shaved off the light, curly beard, and he smiled when she came up to him, the same confident smile he'd shown her last night by her father's gardenpatch out behind the cabin.

She said, 'Walt, don't you know those men could be watching us right this minute?'

He bent, brushed her lips with his mouth, straightened back and continued to confidently smile. 'Perhaps another time,' he said, 'but not today they aren't.'

'How do you know that? And what in the name of heaven are you doing here, this close to the village?'

'One thing at a time,' he said, taking her hand and stepping around the fir tree where shadows made the heat less of a burden. 'I came this close to the village because I was to see you here. That answers one question. As for the other one — one of my grandfather's men isn't able to go tramping about, so he's staying in town keeping an eye on Pete and Sarah Sancroix, as well as your father, and ostensibly on you too. But he missed seeing you leave town with your lady-friends.'

'You are quite sure?'

He stopped near an old, punky stump, took her by the shoulders to seat her upon the stump, and nodded. 'I'm sure. Jacques left a false trail for that sore-legged one to follow around the village.'

'Where is the other one?'

'He has hired an old man to take him out to McLaughlin's cabin, perhaps on the off-chance that I may be back out there hiding. That should take care of him quite well for a day or two.'

Josephine finally smiled. Then she craned back down where the women were still working their way through the berry patch. 'Is that also part of your grand strategy?' she asked.

Walt leaned down to gently lift a heavy coil of dark hair away from Josephine's forehead. 'Not *my* grand strategy love. It seems old Jacques and your father, and some others hereabouts, are delighted to get a chance to match wits with my grandfather's sophisticated thugs.'

She had to smile in spite of her feeling of anxiety. 'Caroline too? Now she's going to be part of something for a change. Walt, you've given Caroline something to talk about that she'll embroider for years to come. When we are as old as she now is, it'll be known as The Epoch of Love's Triumph.'

Josephine laughed, stood up, and when he opened his arms she went up very close to him, tipped back her face to be kissed, and although her fears did not vanish, for that little moment they were most certainly buried deep beneath some other more pleasant and urgent feelings.

14

An Offer to Compromise

That evening at supper she told her father that if he had simply explained that Walter would be out there waiting, she never would have been so reluctant about going off to pick berries.

John, a great believer in the therapeutic benefits of lentil soup in mid-summer when the blood needed thinning, continued to ladle up his meal and for a while did not comment. But after a while he said, 'Well, did you tell him about the meeting with his grandfather's men tomorrow at the store?'

She had. In fact she had gone deeper into the forest with Walter and they had sat on pine needles near a rill of run-off snow-water talking for an hour and a half, before he'd sent her back to the berry-pickers with a kiss, and a promise that they would meet again.

'He said about what you told me this morning — kill time, use up the days, keep those men wondering.'

John finished his soup, smiled at his daughter and reported that he had drifted back down to the store in mid-afternoon to see how Jacques had made out leaving his false trail. John laughed. 'Jacques and the one with the sprained ankle were playing draughts.'

'Draughts?'

'The stranger called out to Jacques. He was very reasonable. He said he knew Jacques was simply keeping him occupied, but that it bothered his sore leg to do that. And since Jacques probably didn't like having to keep moving around in the heat, why didn't they just have a quiet game of draughts. Then each could keep an eye on the other one.'

Josephine laughed, and her father sat across the table with a twinkling pair of dark eyes. He said, 'That would be the way for people to fight wars: Choose sides, and have games of draughts.'

Josephine began moving about the table, removing their soup dishes and bringing over the plates from the oven with meat and squash on them. She even poured more tea before the smile began to fade from her face.

She told her father what Walter had said about the other stranger hiking out to the McLaughlin cabin. John already knew about that.

'Time,' he murmured. 'We use up the time.'

'Those men just aren't that dense,' exclaimed Josephine.

Her father considered his steaming plate of food with pleasure. There is no picture as sweet to the eye of men who cook for themselves as meals cooked for them by women, and that was all, right at the moment, that seemed to occupy John Carbeau.

But after he'd savoured a mouthful he said, 'Well, no one thinks those two men are fools, Josie. But as has been said before — in this country they are not masters, we are.'

It was a pleasantly lulling consideration. Josephine had occasion to fall back on that thought several times before she went to bed that night, but when she rose to prepare breakfast the following morning, conscious of the conference just ahead of her, there seemed a dozen little flaws in the idea.

But John was as unshakeably serene at the breakfast table that morning as he had been the night before. He even joked, saying he thought it probable that old Jacques won at the game of draughts the day before.

Josephine paused outside, when she and her father left the cabin and entered a warm and lovely world of new sunlight and pleasant warmth. She looked off northeastward, but of course he wasn't there, and even if he had been, it was still too far to see him.

John wore his red-checked mackinaw, which was strictly a cold-weather garment. If he noticed the heat he gave

185

no indication of it. Many of the older men wore their mackinaws summer and winter. Not all day long, of course, but at least until the temperature climbed to seventy degrees or better. They seemed to be suspicious of the warm weather lasting.

The walk to the store was pleasant. They encountered people they knew, even stopped once for a cheery little visit with an elderly couple who were out hoeing in their garden patch. It was like stepping back through a slot in time for Josephine; down in Quebec the twentieth century was clamorously present. Up in McLean, which actually wasn't all that distant from Quebec, little had changed for thirty years, and there was much more that hadn't changed for fifty years.

The store, for example, was cool and gloomy, and stocked with an assortment of things people down in Quebec would have smiled about: hunting rifles, steel traps, the old white-striped, maroon blankets, the mantles for coal-oil lamps.

Even Sarah and Pete Sancroix seemed to belong to another time as they welcomed John and Josephine, offering hot tea which Sarah had been brewing in a back room.

The tan-eyed stranger limped in some half an hour later, looking calm and wary. He accepted the chair John gave him with a courteous 'thank you' and even smiled over at Josephine as he said, 'I'd sure like for this to be painless.'

She did not smile as she gave the man look for look and said, 'I don't suppose I can control that. But I *can* control how long I'll sit here.'

There were no other customers, it was too early in the day. They might stroll in later, if the meeting took too long, but at this moment Pete and Sarah were behind the same counter, leaning there, waiting to hear whatever the tan-eyed man had to say. He kept no one waiting very long.

'Miss Carbeau, yesterday at dinner my friend and I talked this thing

187

through, and we came to a decision. Let us see young King for one hour, and if we can't convince him to return to New York with us, we'll leave without him.'

Josephine stared. So did the others. The stranger's tone had been quietly candid. His eyes hadn't wavered. She wavered a little in her resolve to oppose this man regardless of what he said or what attitude he took.

'You already know he won't go voluntarily,' she said. 'He's been a year and more trying to convince his grandfather of that.'

'Okay,' said the large man in the same quiet voice. 'Look; we took a contract to deliver him. That's no secret, and we took it in good faith. But this is getting ridiculous and frustrating . . . You probably know where my partner is . . . '

John nodded his head, speaking for the first time. 'We know. And he's going to have a long trek for nothing.'

The tan-eyed man wasn't annoyed.

'I guessed that and maybe he did too. Still, we've got to keep making the effort; that's what we're being paid for. But when he comes back, you let us talk to young King for one hour, then either we leave with him, or without him, but we'll leave.'

Josephine said, 'I don't trust you. I'd like to, but I can't. You see, I know Walter's grandfather too. He will not give up. Not for another thirty days. After that maybe he'll still fight Walter, but by then it won't matter.'

The stranger evidently knew what she was referring to because he asked no questions and showed no puzzlement as he sat over there gazing at her. Then he crossed his legs, placing the injured ankle up high and holding it with one large hand. 'Do we have a deal, Miss Carbeau? One hour with Walter King — then we leave with or without him?'

'No force?' asked Pete Sancroix, and the tan-eyed man made a slow, tough smile in Pete's direction as he slowly wagged his head back and forth.

'No force, folks. Just a little talk. A little quiet reasoning. That's all. Otherwise we're going to have to drag this thing on and on.' The calm voice briefly paused, and the tawny eyes measured each listening person. 'It's your scrub, up here. Maybe we could cope with that, even, but the people are different. The old man who agreed to guide my friend to the McLaughlin cabin, for instance — how would you have known where they were going if that old guy hadn't told you first? You see what I mean? We're out-classed up here, so what's the point of keeping this up?'

It made sense, and the man was either sincere, or an excellent actor. Pete leaned and rubbed a bristly jaw, looking first at his wife, then at John, and finally at Josephine. He was between-and-betwixt, obviously. So were the others.

It was John who brought up something the others might have overlooked.

'I'm not sure we can find Walter King by tomorrow.'

The tan-eyed man turned a sardonic stare upon old John. 'Mr Carbeau — there's no reason in being sly. If you can't find him *she* can,' he said, nodding towards Josephine. 'McLaughlin will know where he is, even if you don't. But I think all of you know where he is.'

Jacques was absent, and that had been what was in John's thoughts. Jacques was the only one of them who knew from hour to hour or day to day, where Walter was. The tan-eyed man had already deduced that. Perhaps Jacques had said something the day before during their game of draughts to give the stranger this impression, but whether this was true or not, they were all more or less positive Jacques was the key.

Pete sighed, scratched his head and glanced indifferently out of the window where sunlight bounced off the dusty roadway with eye-stinging intensity.

'You go now,' he told the tan-eyed man. 'Let us discuss it.'

The stranger got gingerly to his feet, settled most of his weight on his sound leg, and turned a final look upon Josephine. 'There's nothing underhanded about my offer. Win or lose we can't very well go back to Mr King in New York and say we gave up without even talking to his grandson.'

The man shifted his weight and went lightly limping out of the store with four pairs of eyes watching him out of sight. Then Sarah said, 'Josie, don't trust those men. They know they can't find Walter unless one of us leads them to him, and that's exactly what this one is trying to make you do.'

The beautiful girl looked at her father, but John was using a thick thumb to tamp shag-tobacco into a stubby little old pipe, and neglected to catch her look of appeal.

Pete rubbed his jaw and scowled, clearly pulled first one way then another way. In the end he said, 'Suppose the man is telling the truth? If they couldn't talk Walter into leaving with them, then they would leave, and that would solve everything.'

Finally, John spoke up. 'It is up to you,' he told his daughter, dark eyes a little hard and cold. 'If you decide to bring these people together, then I think you had better have them meet right here in the store, or at our cabin. That way we can be sure they only talk. Pete, Jacques and I will be handy to be sure of that.'

Josephine voiced her one major objection to the meeting. 'They can't possibly say anything that will change Walt's mind. He's as stubborn as his grandfather is, and if he hasn't given up before now, he won't change just because the three of them talk. Anyway, he doesn't want to see these men, so why should I ask him to?'

Sarah smiled, finally, the first show of expression she had made in an hour. 'What do you care what those men have to tell Grandfather King when they return to New York? Let them go back with their tails between their legs.'

A carload of vacationers pulled up to the sidewalk in front of the house and began piling out of the car with a small boy springing from foot to foot looking to be in anguish. He grabbed his mother's hand and tugged her down so he could whisper, and afterwards the woman, with a look of exasperation, turned and craned in all directions. Pete Sancroix sighed a soft curse under his breath and started for the front door to point out to the woman with the anguished little boy how to get around behind the store where the bathrooms were.

John and Josephine rose to depart. Sarah went towards the door with them to say she thought they should discuss their problem with Jacques, so he could go to discuss it with Walter.

That was the only decision they

really arrived at, and it was made as those vacationers swarmed into the store breaking around the talking people, heading towards the candy counter.

15

A Sunshiny Morning

Jacques first heard of that meeting the night before it had taken place. He and Walter were having a leisurely supper in an old cave which was about nine miles from the McLaughlin cabin, and which was another two miles northeast of McLean.

Walter expressed the idea that his grandfather's men had devised some kind of scheme, and Jacques nodded while eating dinner. Later, he said if Walt wished they could leave before sunrise the following morning and be in the village in time for the meeting, but Walter had declined. For one thing, Jacques had been up very late the night before and needed some rest. For another, as he said, it didn't matter if they held meetings every day for the next month, as long as he wasn't involved nothing could be resolved.

A little later, offering proof that in fact he was tired, old Jacques rolled into his blanket, turned his back to the little fire, and within moments was sound asleep.

The cave was quite warm, even along towards dawn after the fire had died to grey ash and coals. Walter slept as though he were down in New York in his own bed at home. In fact Jacques had the coffee boiling before Walt even opened his eyes. Boiling coffee was a mighty good titillater of latent appetites. Walt blinked over at the fire, at the cross-legged figure of Jacques, then he grinned, yawned, and sat up to stretch. 'Like the Boston-Hilton,' he said.

Jacques grinned. 'Eat fast because we'll have to hurry. Two miles isn't very far, but it will take an hour or more, and it's already seven o'clock. Maybe they will be meeting again.'

Obviously Jacques had been thinking, and had decided to go, and let the others tell him the results of that meeting the day before. Possibly as a second-thought it had occurred to him there could be another meeting. As he said when they were having their coffee, 'Those men your grandfather hired can walk here and there; they can try bribes even, and they can even try finding us on their own, but whatever they are up to, they need you, don't they? Well, we had better watch them a little closer, but not necessarily let them watch us.'

'You think they'll finally offer enough money to tempt someone?' asked Walter, and old Jacques finished his coffee, smiled at the younger man, got to his feet without answering that question, and walked out of the cave into the fresh new golden-lighted day. All he said for the next half hour as they started away from the cave and until they were well on their way, was that a morning as wonderful as this one was, made a man feel as though he had just shed thirty years of his life as easily as a snake sheds its winter skin.

They were in no hurry, partly because it was indeed such a delightful day, partly because they did not have any great distance to cover. But they did not tarry either, for as Jacques had pointed out at the cave, they had risen rather late, and possibly they would want to reach the village before anything occurred, which turned out to be a pretty fair guess, for as they came out of the scrub north of town they saw the blue-eyed stranger talking to a wizened, dark old man not very far from where the last cabins stood and where the roadway petered out into several broad, meandering trails.

Jacques waited until those two separated, but instead of motioning for Walter to follow the blue-eyed man, he turned with a sly wink and led off in the direction of the blue-eyed man's guide.

They intercepted the old Cree where

it was convenient to do so, and where sheds and other outbuildings shielded them from the sight of the other man, who had gone trudging down towards the main part of town after paying off his guide.

The old Cree, when he looked up and found himself intercepted, slowly and broadly smiled at Jacques. 'Your axe had fallen out of the tree near the woodpile,' he said. 'So I put it back before the wood-rats chewed up the handle for the salt.'

Walter grinned. The old man had told them where he had been without waiting to be questioned. He also said, 'It was a good walk, even if the man I guided didn't think so. Even sleeping in the forest was pleasant.'

Jacques nodded. 'He paid you?'

'Yes. Enough. He didn't talk much and he didn't smile at all. But he walked right along with me and he paid plenty for a guide. Just once, when I was sitting on the porch of your cabin eating an apple, did he act as though he wasn't happy. He said I had probably known there was nothing out here even when I agreed to guide him.'

Jacques and Walt exchanged a look, the younger man smiling, the older man showing no actual smile, only a faint, sardonic twinkle. Then Jacques asked the other man if the stranger had mentioned needing a guide again.

The answer was half a shrug. 'Not exactly, but he said something — he said he knew a man who owned some dogs.'

As the three men stood there in morning warmth looking at one another, they all understood what might have prompted that thought, and eventually, just before the old Cree walked away, he said, 'Sooner or later someone would think of that, wouldn't they?'

Walt and Jacques started back towards the northerly terminus of the main roadway, each busy with his private thoughts. It was Walter who spied the limping man first, and threw out an arm to halt his companion. A limping man always caught someone's attention, and this particular man accomplished that because, apart from his uneven gait, there were no other strollers heading in the same direction — towards the Carbeau cabin.

Jacques watched the man soberly, with his mind elsewhere, and just before the limping man turned to pass from sight towards the Carbeau yard, Jacques said, 'Well, they aren't going to give up, I guess, and it will cost a lot of money to import dogs from the States.' Then he turned, thinly smiling. 'But it's nothing much to worry about. Years ago I remember when the Mounted Police brought dogs to McLean to hunt down a man who had been killing caribou when he shouldn't have been. I was a boy at the time but I remember what they did; five different men went and bathed in the creeks, then put on the wanted man's clothes, and started out together. Where one stopped, after a few miles, another man would go on. Five of them did that in relays. The constables wore out, their dogs got sore-footed, and the fugitive was already half way southward to Quebec before the constables figured out what was happening.' Jacques's sunk-set eyes brightened in recollection, then he roused himself and turned, saying perhaps they ought to go down to the Carbeau place before much more time passed.

When they had passed through several patches of sturdy weeds and had the rear of the Carbeau cabin in sight, there was a thin trickle of smoke rising from the stove-pipe. Walter said, 'Sitting in the kitchen having coffee,' and Jacques nodded.

They moved in on an angle approaching the house from the direction of John's garden-patch. It was while they were still in the corn-rows that they saw the blue-eyed man come ambling into the yard in front of the house, from the direction of the centre of town. He looked tired, hadn't shaved nor changed his clothing, so in all probability after he had gone in search of his friend, he'd either come directly back to the Carbeau place on a hunch, or someone may have told him where his companion was.

Jacques said, 'I will go in. You stay out here. If you should be in there, I'll send Josephine out here for you. Otherwise, wait.'

Walter seemed about to argue, but Jacques strode forth with a swift step, came around the rear of the house just as the blue-eyed man ambled up to the front, and Jacques knocked first.

John admitted McLaughlin while Josephine went through to the front of the house to admit the other visitor. Before she returned, and with Pete Sancroix sitting at the kitchen table nursing a cup of black coffee, John said, 'Where have you been?' to McLaughlin. 'We were expecting you last night?'

The other man at the kitchen table was the tan-eyed, limping stranger. He cocked a sceptical eye at Jacques but said nothing because at that moment Josephine returned from the front of the house with the other man.

There was only one person absent from among those who had attended the earlier meeting: Sarah Sancroix. That left Josephine as the only woman.

The unshaven man dropped wearily into a chair, looked sardonically around as Josie went to get him a cup of coffee, and said, 'Mace, did you explain to them?'

The tan-eyed man nodded. 'Yeah. Just one hour or less with young King.'

The stranger glanced up as Josephine woodenly leaned to put the coffee before him. He said, 'Thanks. You know — young King is very lucky.' He didn't amplify that. He really didn't have to. Josephine went round to her father's side of the table, sat and waited, as they were all doing, for whatever the weary man would say next.

But it was his companion, the man called Mace, who spoke; he reiterated everything he had suggested the day before, and he wound it up with a shrug and a growl. 'I guess you folks didn't believe me.' What he meant, of course, was that Walter wasn't there.

No one bothered to explain they hadn't been able to get word to Walter. The blue-eyed man was revived a little by the coffee. He fished under his jacket for a cigar and lit it. That seemed to heighten his morale even more. He said, 'Look; I've been walking since four o'clock this morning, and you people knew it was a wild goose chase right from the start. Okay. I'm not a sore-head. We expected opposition before we came here. But it's not going to be all one-sided. From now on we'll hunt King down our own way. I guess we should have done that right from the start.'

'I thought you just wanted to talk to him,' said Josephine.

The cigar-smoking man eyed her critically through grey smoke, his pale gaze steady, and hard. 'We do. But if you people persist in blocking our efforts, why then you don't leave us much alternative but to be a little rough.'

'That,' said John Carbeau, 'wouldn't be very wise.'

The tan-eyed one shrugged. 'Tom just put it on the line. Yesterday, I tried to do that too. Look folks, I told you — we can't go back empty-handed. You don't know Mr King. We've got to show how hard we tried, if we fail. But we don't like failing, so when we try to be reasonable and you folks just fight back — well . . . '

Pete Sancroix was scowling now. 'I think what I'll do is send for a constable. We probably should have done that a week ago.'

Mace wasn't very impressed. 'Go ahead and bring in your cop. What do you tell him? That two men from New York want to *talk* to another man from New York. I doubt if that's a crime, even in Canada.'

For the first time Jacques spoke. He

was sitting like an old oak carving, his black stare flicking only when different people spoke. 'Do you carry guns?' he asked.

The blue-eyed man smiled and shook his head. 'You've been reading too many detective stories about life in the States. We don't carry guns or use them, or even need them. We're not hoodlums, mister, we're private investigators hired to locate a missing man.'

'And abduct him,' murmured Josie.

Mace curved his lips at her in a mirthless smile. 'I've already explained to you, lady, we don't want to abduct your boy-friend.'

'Then how would you get him out of Canada, since he doesn't want to go back with you?'

'Lady, all we want is to talk to him. He's been gone a year, almost. How does he know he doesn't want to leave here and go back with us?'

Jacques leaned over, whispered something to Josephine, and when she turned to stare, the old man ignored her and said, 'You can talk to him. But I want to tell you something; if you have lied . . . ' Old Jacques lifted the right side of his old jacket. There was a shoulder-holstered revolver under there. He did not finish his remark and no one expected him to.

Josie got up and turned away without a word to any of them. She went outside through the backdoor, and the man smoking the cigar finished his cup of coffee watching her depart with a speculative, narrowed look.

After that, the five men sat silently at the table, watching each other. It was the stranger called Mace speaking to his companion, who finally broke the hush. 'Tom, I think we're beginning to get through.'

Whatever that meant, Mace did not explain, but it was fair to assume it meant that Mace had guessed what Jacques had whispered, and where Josephine had gone.

16

The Bombshell!

For Walter the wait was long and annoying. As he told Josephine when he stepped forth to greet her, there was no reason for him to fear a confrontation.

Her reply was gentle but pointed. 'There are two of them, Walter, and they don't look quite like Boy Scouts to me.'

He kissed her lightly on the cheek to bring a smile, and it worked, although the smile was less than radiant. 'I wish we could just turn our backs and walk away,' she sighed.

'Very soon,' he averred. Then he turned brisk again. 'What is it they want?'

'To talk to you. That's all they said they wanted. The man who doesn't limp just returned from Jacques's cabin this morning. He looks tired.'

Walter knew these things but did not comment on them, instead he reached to place a dark lock of her curly hair back away from where it had tumbled, and glanced thoughtfully towards the house. 'Let's go,' he said, then hesitated. 'I wish I knew if they'd contacted my grandfather lately.'

'Why?'

'Well, he didn't know where I was. That is, not *specifically*, but if they told him you can bet that if they said they were having trouble, he'd respond.'

'You mean with more men?'

Walter looked down at her lifted face. 'I don't know. That's what I'm wary of.'

She said, 'Then don't go in there. We can take my father's car and — .'

'Love, I've just run my last mile,' he broke in to say, then he bent, brushed her lips lightly, turned her and started towards the house still holding her hand.

At the kitchen door he reached without hesitation, flung the door inward and met the impassive stares of those men at the table. He nodded and everyone excepting Pete Sancroix and old Jacques nodded back. Then he waited for Josephine to precede him inside, and afterwards closed the door.

It was silent for a moment, until Josephine stepped away to approach the stove and see if the coffee pot needed re-filling. It did, so while she was busy at the tap John Carbeau got another chair and bobbed his head at it, inviting Walter King to be seated.

Finally, the tan-eyed man made a slow, rather craggy smile. 'You wintered good,' he said, without sounding very hostile. It was an almost casual greeting and did not imply how much difficulty and inconvenience the limping man had survived searching for Walter.

But it was the blue-eyed one, no longer smoking his cigar, who got down to business. He didn't even offer so much as a whimsical greeting the way his friend had done.

'Look, Mr King, your grandfather simply wants to see you, to talk with you. If you'd given him a chance last year it would have saved all of us a lot of jumping around.'

Walter shifted his attention to the blue-eyed man. 'I've spoken with my grandfather a dozen times,' he said, 'and it has always been the same. Maybe you know it, maybe you don't, but very successful business men are never very good compromisers. And compromise always has to be from the other fellow. Well, that's where the stalemate is. I'm not going back until I'm good and ready to, and if my grandfather wants to see me, he can come here. Or write a letter. If it's urgent he could even call me on the telephone down at Sancroix's store.'

The blue-eyed man was respectfully silent until Walter had finished speaking, then said, 'Would you step outside with me where we can discuss all this privately?'

Walter slowly shook his head. 'Right here will be fine.'

The blue-eyed man smiled. 'We're not planning on kidnapping you.'

'I don't think you are,' said Walter. 'But these people have earned the right to hear what's said.'

The blue-eyed man nodded slightly. 'That they have, Mr King; they've bucked us every inch of the way, and your grandfather didn't like that very much.'

'Then you've talked to him?'

'Couple of days ago. He said to tell you something: Unless you come back before the month is out, he is going to disinherit you.'

Walter nodded. 'I'd have thought he'd have done that long ago.'

'Let me finish, Mr. King. He will disinherit you — *and your brother.*'

Walter stared. 'My brother? Sanford's had nothing at all to do with this disagreement.'

'Well, maybe not, Mr King, but your grandfather seems to think you'll want to protect your brother from being kicked out flat broke.'

Finally, it was clear to everyone listening why the strangers had wanted to speak to Walter. They had no blandishments to offer, only a threat. Just how much of a threat it was could be seen in Walter's paleness, in the slow darkening of his gaze as he stared at his grandfather's men, and finally by the way he slumped a little at a time in the chair, saying nothing.

The blue-eyed man went on. 'Look; speaking as someone who is interested in fulfilling an assignment and being well paid for that, but as someone who just can't quite fathom all this vindictiveness, Mr King, explain one thing to me. You are of age. Miss Carbeau is of age. Now what can one old man do to force you into doing what he wants, that the two of you can't just simply out-wait?'

Walter's mouth twisted into an ugly grimace. 'That's not a very perceptive question,' he replied. 'You have just given an example of what one old man can do. And he'll do it, too, and a whole lot more, the minute I go to meet him. If he would ruin my brother, who has knuckled under and has worked hard for the syndicate ever since leaving school, to get at me, what do you think he is capable of doing to me, for having defied him this long?'

'Well, hell,' exclaimed the big man. 'He can't do very much.'

'You are terribly wrong, and obviously you don't know him very well, either. He doesn't want me to marry. Not just Miss Carbeau, not to marry *anyone* — until and unless he finds someone *he* might figure would bring even greater power to the family holdings. If he decides King Syndicate is big enough, rich enough and powerful enough, then he wouldn't want me to marry, ever.' Walter leaned forward. 'Would you want to live a life like that — absolutely dependent from day to day, on what one cold-blooded old man wants?'

The tan-eyed man kept probing his

injured ankle without looking up as he said, 'Mr King, we're getting away from the topic. What Tom hasn't told you yet is that we are to ring up your grandfather no later than the end of this week and give him your answer. That's why we were so insistent about talking to you.' The tawny eyes lifted and settled upon Walter's pale face. 'Either we report that you refuse to come, and in that case — well — I suppose Mr King can do what he says about your brother — can't he?'

For a moment no one moved. Behind Josephine the coffee-pot began to perk cheerily, which was the only sound in the kitchen. Finally Jacques McLaughlin's chair squeaked as he shifted position, turning to gaze at Walter.

Pete Sancroix's swarthy countenance was pinched down hard in an unpleasant expression, while from beneath a jutting brow he coldly examined the two men across the table.

John Carbeau smiled at his white-faced daughter. 'Coffee would taste good,' he murmured, and it sounded incongruous in that environment of dark swirling emotions.

Josephine turned almost automatically to pick up the pot and take it to the table where those empty cups sat. She made hardly any sound, even when pouring each cup full.

Finally, the blue-eyed man, perhaps made restless or uneasy by the stare of those bright black eyes opposite, said, 'Mr King goes back, talks with his grandfather, and comes back.' He shrugged thick shoulders and if he hadn't dropped his eyes he might have brought it off, but to the others it was not convincing.

Pete said, 'You have to be a damned hypocrite to say what you just said, mister.'

At once both the large men straightened in their chairs. This, evidently, was an attitude they were experienced in facing.

Jacques shook his head at them very slowly. 'It won't do any good,' he said quietly. 'If you raise a hand in this house — it won't be very good for you.'

The large men gazed at old McLaughlin. Whether they were remembering the hidden revolver or were simply thinking of something else, perhaps the odds of four to one, or possibly something altogether different such as an admonition against violence, no one knew but they, and for as long as it took Josephine to finish with the coffee neither of them spoke or moved, but after that the blue-eyed one gave his head a little tough shake, then spoke.

'Yeah. Well; I guess none of us keeps skating around the thin ice forever without getting a toe wet, do we? Anyway, let's forget that kind of talk. My partner and I have been following orders. We are still following them. Now it's up to Mr King.' With that the two men stood up, the tan-eyed one making a slight grimace as his injured ankle let him know it was down there.

'Mr King? You've got a couple of days. I'm sorry how it has to be, but we work for your grandfather. Incidentally, you won't have to hide any more. My partner and I'll be around, but only until the end of the week. Like we already told these people — either you leave with us, or we leave without you. In any case, I'll be tickled pink to get out of this town by the end of the week. If you want to talk, look us up at the boarding-house south of town from the general store.'

John rose to escort the large men to the front door. Out there the three of them looked a little awkwardly at one another, then the blue-eyed man ducked his head and growled.

'Thanks for the hospitality. The coffee was very good.'

John remained in the doorway watching the large men walk across his yard and out into the street, heading for the centre of town. Then he closed the door and went silently back to the kitchen.

Walter and Josephine were gone.

Pete said with a little shrug, 'They needed fresh air. Let them go.' He reached and peered into his cup, found some coffee remaining and lifted it to his lips.

John sat down opposite Jacques McLaughlin in the chair the man called Tom, the blue-eyed one, had vacated. 'Well, now he doesn't have to hide, does he?'

'Hiding would be easier than what he has to do now,' said Jacques. 'I knew a lot of old men before I became one myself, but never one like his grandfather. Does he think he will live forever? That he can do anything he likes?'

'He's doing it, isn't he?' growled Pete. 'Tell me, Jacques, what would you do in Walter's boots?'

McLaughlin didn't answer but the expression on his face showed that he was wrestling with an answer.

John went digging around in his pockets for the little stubby pipe and his pouch. As he loaded up he shot both his companions a look. 'It wouldn't do any good to talk to that old man. I thought about that out at the front door.'

'And it wouldn't even help to bribe those big men,' said Pete. 'Even if they could be bribed.'

'So Walter must make his decision.'

'It's not that he is to be stood up and shot,' mumbled Jacques. But he didn't sound very convincing. 'He must not let that old man ruin his brother.'

Pete and John looked at old Jacques, and McLaughlin looked straight back.

'Josephine and her young man will simply have to go on waiting. What else is there for them? How could they look at each other if they married, and that old man ruined the brother?' Jacques reached for his hat and stood up a trifle stiffly. 'I never heard of such an old man before.' He jerked his head at Sancroix. 'Let's go down to your store.

I want to buy a cigar and sit in the shade and think.'

John Carbeau also went along with the other two, leaving the house empty, and redolent of that cigar the blue-eyed man had smoked.

It was past noon now, although none of the three elderly men seemed aware of it as they trudged along, tall, lank Jacques McLaughlin between the shorter men.

17

The Riddle Becomes a Fact

McLaughlin had stated what seemed to be the obvious course, and Josephine, who hadn't been there to hear McLaughlin's remarks, re-stated them as she and Walter King walked out a slight way from the village heading for one of those low, insignificant rolls of land that had bushes and trees on its low eminence. Only her statements were not as dry, they were more soft and despairing.

'This time there is no limit,' she told Walter. 'Before, it was possible to see an end, someday, to all the waiting. But this time he's left it up in the air. He'll destroy your brother if you marry — if you don't come back to New York by the end of the week — and the question of what happens after you go back is left wide open.'

Walter did not look down at her but kept strolling through the warm afternoon out towards the little low hillock. 'If it works he'll have exactly the club over my head he's always wanted. Every time I go up against him, all he has to do is threaten to ruin Sanford. It worked here, with you, so he'll be certain it will always work.'

'What an incredible old man,' she murmured. 'Doesn't he fear anything?'

Walter finally looked down. 'Fear?'

'You know what I mean. Doesn't he fear some kind of retribution?'

'Oh. I don't think he has ever feared anything in his life. I know for a fact that when he finally retired and went west to live on his estate everyone at the top including my father, was delighted. Of course I was just a kid, and I was supposed to have a grandfather just like every other kid, so my father never spoke against the old man, but I could sense things. No, love, the old man not only never feared anything, he is the one who has worked hard to *be* feared.'

She said, 'We don't have to talk about him. Tell me of your brother.'

'Five years older than I am. Sanford is also scared to death of grandfather. But he was a brilliant corporation attorney, and he loves every minute of being what he is — a very rich and powerful executive in one of America's most powerful family enterprises. So you see, when grandfather sent word he'd ruin Sanford, he meant it both figuratively and literally, because if he threw Sanford out and bankrupted him, it would also break my brother's heart.'

'Your brother sounds as though he may develop into a man like your grandfather,' murmured Josephine, and taking his hand led him around the stony base of their low hill where she knew there was a path through the wild grape and pine-bush.

He denied it instantly. 'Oh no, not Sandy. He loves power and wealth and comfort. He even likes making those big decisions — and he's very good at all of it — but you'd have to know him to realize he'd never be like grandfather if he lived to be a hundred.'

She turned and saw the warmth in his face. 'You are fond of your brother.'

Walter nodded. 'He has a terrific sense of humour. He's a good sport. All my life when I got down in the dumps Sandy came along and pulled me up out of them. You'll have to get to know him, love. You'll think there's no one like Sandy.'

At the top of the gravely knoll several shaggy old unkempt pines grew, too crooked and low-limbed to ever have been coveted by loggers, and for the same reason not wanted by cutters of autumn firewood. There was also more wild, or mock, grape at the crest. Because there was little actual soil, only sand and stony gravel, not much else grew. At least right then, in mid-summer, but as he looked about, commenting on the barrenness of the place with its silence, pine-scent and tree-shade, she pointed to a crumbly outcropping of lichened-coloured flaky rock and told him every year snow-flowers appeared there for several weeks in spring. They were a rare, delicate, blood-red plant and died-back as soon as the top few inches of earth dried out, and as soon as the real heat came.

Her father, in showing her that place as a child, had smilingly told her that the oldtime Cree believed, or at least professed to believe, that any wish made upon the scarlet petals of a snow-flower would be answered, but only after the plant was no longer earth-bound, and could soar to heaven with its messages.

He smiled. 'Too bad we didn't come here a couple of months ago.'

Shadows were slanting downward from the hazy west now, striking the village on an angle and smoothing out every rough corner, each old rut and furrow. Now and then a sound, distance-softened, drifted out to their shady place; the bark of a dog, the yelp of a boisterous child, the half-lost soft echo of a bell.

As they stood looking back, she said, 'Walter, of course I'll wait, but I don't like what I'm thinking.'

He slid an arm round her waist. 'We'll be married, Josie.'

She was shocked. 'You'd do that to your brother?'

'No. We'll be married secretly.'

She kept looking up at him, and after a bit, when she resumed her study of the distant village, she shook her head. 'Not like that, Walter. Not like we're ashamed of it. When I marry you I'll want the whole world to know. I'll want to see Sarah Sancroix smile and have old Jacques smile, and listen to Pete and my father sing one of those old *chansons*. A good marriage here in McLean gives everyone an excuse to celebrate. And they do it. They eat and have games, drink and dance and sing.' Her eyes glowed and a soft smile shaped her lips. 'Even if we don't live

here, Walter, we'll always come back
— and the people are our friends.'
Finally she lifted her face again. 'We
aren't ashamed — are we?'

He hugged her close. 'No, we're not
ashamed. We'll never be that. I love
you so much, Josie. But there is no
other way.'

'Yes. We wait.'

He protested. 'I've *been* waiting. I
waited when I was in school and
I waited afterwards. Even after my
brother got to be one of the chief
executives, I had to keep on waiting.
And now this — this past year which
has been hardest of all. Sweetheart, I'm
a man, not a child. I deserve a wife and
a family.'

'And your brother — whom you love
so much — what does he deserve,
Walter?'

Of course there was no answer to
one question without there also being
a bitter answer to the other one. He
held her close and said nothing.

She clung to him and cried without

moving or making a sound, and when they finally moved apart as shadows thickened she kept her face averted although their fingers were interlocked, and said, 'I think I'll go to talk to your grandfather, Walter. No, I'm not going to get down on my knees to him, or scold him or be defiant. I just want to hear him tell me why he doesn't want you to be a normal man.'

'I can answer that and save you the humiliation of having him refuse to see you — which is exactly what he will do. He has no feelings for anything but the syndicate. He spent all his life making it bigger and it's all that's left in this world for him. He will tell you that he's either going to shape my brother and me in the same image, or get rid of us and find someone else to replace him. Josie, you can't reason with him. I know, love; I've been trying ever since I was in college. You'll want to cry when you walk away from him, because he hasn't been a real human being in fifty years.' He took her over where a crumbly old boulder stood and sat her down there. 'Don't go. If you do, you'll return feeling worse than you feel now.'

She kept looking up at him. 'Walter, we've already had to wait too long.'

He seemed to sense the finality in her look and voice, because he suddenly dropped to her side and, taking her face in both hands, leaned to press her lips lightly with his mouth, and to say afterwards, 'I know, Josie. I had all last winter to think about it. I'll go back with those men at the end of the week.'

She stiffened.

'Let me finish, love. I'll go back with them, but not to see *him*, to explain to Sandy what the alternatives are.'

'So he will have to make the decision, Walter?'

'I don't know any other way, Josie.'

'He has a family?'

'Yes.'

'And he likes his position?'

'Yes.'

'Then you can't do that to him, Walter. You'd be asking him to do something you have no right to ask of anyone; to give up his whole life for us.' She blinked rapidly but the brightness shimmered in her eyes nontheless. 'If he refused — do you see what it would do to you — to us?'

His hands dropped and his shoulders slumped. 'Josie, don't tell me all the things I *can't* do, or that I *shouldn't* do. Tell me something we *can* do.'

'Keep on loving each other, Walter,' she murmured and leaned her face against his shoulder, eyes closed, teeth locked against the anguish that tore at her heart and spirit.

They were silent for a long time, and even after they rose and started along the edge of the little land-swell, heading for the downward trail, they had nothing to say to each other.

The moon soared from below some distant, broken peaks, not full and not even giving much light, but huge and curved and mysterious, and a horned owl flew between them and it, making a silent, large outline. She waited, watching the big bird, and squeezed his fingers but still said nothing.

He pointed down where the village glowed with soft light. Electricity had come to McLean many years earlier but for two reasons a good many people still chose to use coal-oil lamps; in wintertime the transmission lines broke frequently under loads of freezing snow and high winds. Also, not everyone had been so delighted at the arrival of this modern magic that they'd felt impelled to wire their cabins.

It was easy to pick out which were the whiter, more glaring electric lights from the more orangy, less glaring oil-lamps. The contrast was rather like the shades of a rainbow; pleasant, interesting, peaceful.

She led the way back down the old trail. At the bottom where they emerged through wild-grape scrub and had one of the broader trails ahead of them, leading back to the village, she turned and smiled at him in the moonlight.

'We have each other, and we have health.'

'And McLean,' he said, as though he were thinking they could always meet here, but there was also a detectable drag to the words as though he knew better. As though he had said that only to reassure her when he knew perfectly well that his grandfather's shadow would always be between them.

She kept looking at him. He was tall and broad and fair, and although a man would not only never think of the word for another man, and wouldn't even use it if he thought of it, to her he was — beautiful.

'Will you go to see those men at the boarding-house tonight?' she asked.

'Tomorrow maybe. There's still plenty of time. I thought that maybe tonight, if you liked, we'd go together to a café and have dinner in plain sight of everyone. I guess you could say that's my first flying of a flag of defiance.'

She nodded, thinking past that first flag because she was, like Sarah Sancroix, a very practical person, and took his hand again as they started slowly down towards the village.

She wasn't hungry. So didn't remember when she'd eaten last, but she felt no desire for food now at all. Still, she would go with him, and she would eat.

Someone began ringing a flute-toned bell. He asked why and she explained that because the air was so clear mothers summoned their children with bells, whose sound carried a surprisingly long way, and that also, each bell had a different ring: children learned their particular ring above all the other bell-sounds.

He smiled and drew her close with an arm round her middle. 'We'll have a bell someday,' he said, and she nodded her head without looking up and without speaking. Maybe, but more than likely they would not. Fate in the form of a distant old man was decreeing otherwise very powerfully.

18

A Long, Gentle Night

Pete occasionally took Sarah to dinner at one particular restaurant in McLean, but the occasion had to be something very memorable, such as their anniversary — which he never remembered but which she never forgot — or a birthday, his or hers, and of course when the holidays arrived, or one of their children came home, but if all these events sounded as though the Sancroixs ate out often, it was misleading. Like most men married a long while, Pete was so accustomed to one woman's cooking no other cooking, and certainly no restaurant cooking, ever pleased him.

They were leaving the café this particular night when they encountered Josephine and Walter. It wasn't late, actually, the Sancroixs just hadn't gone home after closing the store. In fact there was still a faint pale glow overhead as though daylight were only hiding, but that was part of what was involved in living so close to the world of the Northern Lights, because there was also a moon, some stars, and down the far curve of the sky, a deep and endless purple.

Pete nodded at Walter with a querying kind of a smile. 'Those men are inside,' he said, meaning of course the two hirelings of Walter's grandfather. Then Pete shrugged. 'Not that it matters, eh?'

Sarah's dark-liquid gaze looked past both men to Josie. 'Jacques is with your father. I think he will be staying in town for a while.'

That seemed to remind Pete of something. 'The postman left a letter for you at the store. If you wish we can walk down there now and get it.'

Walter wasn't concerned. He would call for the letter in the morning. After that, the couples parted, Pete and Sarah to pace towards home down the bland night, Walt and Josie to enter the restaurant, which was a large log room, cheery and bright, and usually about half full, as it was this particular night. At once they both saw Grandfather King's men over across the room at a small round table that sported a gay checked tablecloth of red and white gingham.

If those two saw Josie and her companion they gave no indication of it. Not right then at any rate.

The food was plain fare and served in hefty amounts, the tea was strong enough to serve as a substitute for embalming fluid, and the restaurant's atmosphere was uncomplicated, relaxed, and friendly. Most of the people eating there, or serving the meals, knew Josie, and either waved or smiled or called a greeting, and they also took a candid and lively interest in her companion, for McLean was a village, and people had ways of hearing things about other people in villages they never heard in cities.

'You are being dissected,' she told him, tenderly smiling. 'The women are thinking how beautiful you are, and the men are thinking how large you are.'

'Does anyone ever take an interest in how *dumb* I can be?'

They ordered roast beef, potatoes, blueberry pie and tea. There was no salad, and when the bread came it turned out to be thick chunks off a golden-crusted round loaf. Like rye, Walter said, only white.

She tasted it. 'Sourdough bread. When I was a child there were still some of the oldtimers around who called it French bread and wouldn't touch it because they didn't like the French.'

He smiled, and if she was trying to prevent both of them from thinking of their hopeless dilemma, she was succeeding, because as he tasted the bread he said, 'Frankly, I can't see a whole lot of difference between Crees and Frenchmen.'

'There isn't any, really, but I guess no one likes to think they are losing their identity. There probably aren't any fullblood Crees left, and those curly-headed kids you see around town,' she winked at him. 'Indians never have curly hair. On the other hand the French were never tall, but even Sarah is as tall, maybe even a little taller, than Pete.'

By moving her eyes just a little she could include that yonder table with the checkered, red gingham tablecloth in her view. She saw the man with the sprained ankle gazing at them, but dropped her glance to her food and said nothing.

Later when those two big men over across the room had finished their dinner and rose to depart, they ambled among the other tables and stopped where Walter could see them.

The blue-eyed one, who always seemed to be the dominant personality of that pair, smiled with a show of actual amiability. 'Tried to reach your grandfather tonight, but couldn't get through. That probably won't make you feel happy, Mr King, but the reason I tried to get him was to see if maybe we couldn't arrange for a little delay; say maybe another three or four days.'

It was actually a kindness, although Josephine studied the big man with suspicion and mistrust stamped across her face. Walter nodded. 'I'm obliged,' he said. 'I'll be around to see you in the morning.'

After the two large men had departed Walter leaned on the table. 'Grandfather goes to bed every night promptly at eight o'clock, and if a world-war broke out, or a second deluge came in the night, if anyone awakened him to sound the alarm, he'd fire them on the spot.'

Josephine sighed and returned to her meal. It was hard to imagine such a man as Grandfather King. Of course the reason it was hard was because people always had to fit other people into specific moulds; if there was no mould, then people shook their heads or sighed with bafflement. And without much doubt, although the world had plenty of hard-hearted and cold-blooded men in it, Grandfather King was more than just that; he was harder and colder, and less understandable; at least to a beautiful Cree girl.

Caroline Laughlin came in with another single woman. She looked profoundly surprised to see Josephine eating there, where everyone could see them, with Walter. But Caroline strolled past towards the recently-vacated table with the red gingham cloth on it, and only paused to smile.

Josie smiled, following the older woman's figure with her dark glance. 'She's eating her heart out with curiosity. Poor Caroline.'

Walter finally finished with his meal. He'd eaten a fair amount, probably twice as much as Josie had eaten but then she hadn't been hungry when they'd entered the place. He turned his head slightly to gaze around. He knew some of the people in the restaurant; that is, he had seen them either in the village or out somewhere in the valley, and while not knowing their names, had a vague notion about who they were.

Of course *he* was known to them, for as Josephine had intimated, he was something of a minor celebrity, or to put it another way, those other people were many and indigenous, while he was only one person, and a newcomer.

Josephine, seeing his interested glances, murmured a name here, a little background material there. For example, that particularly dark, powerful man over near the far counter, was the village constable — that is, he was empowered by the Town Council to maintain order within the village limits, but he was not entitled to designate himself a 'constable' anywhere else because that infringed upon the sovereignty of the Mounted Police — the 'redcoats' — who brooked no nonsense in matters of police jurisdiction.

The woman wolfing down food over across the room with Caroline Laughlin, was named Hetty Pacquin. Her first name was actually Hespeth but no one had ever been able to spell it the same way twice, including poor Hetty, so it had ceased being used, in official matters, years ago.

Walter smiled after a while, and slowly drifted his gaze back to Josephine. He didn't say it, but he admired the way she was keeping things light and cheerful between them. Whether she knew it or not, she was keeping them both looking happy, and that would not go unnoticed by the other diners.

Finally he leaned to cover one of her hands with a large palm and said, 'I'll tell you something; if only Grandfather were human, I'd take you down to meet him. He'd think you just about the most special thing he'd ever met.'

'An Indian?' she asked quietly, but

smiling slightly because that hadn't mattered for a hundred years or longer in western Canada or Northwestern America.

Walter shrugged. 'If he were human he'd rush out and have a mink tipi made for you.'

'We never lived in tipis. Always in wooden houses — paleface.'

They grinned and were happy, without a single thought of anything but one another for a moment. She liked it so much that way that even though her strong streak of practicality persevered she ignored it.

He counted out the money, left it along with a sizable tip beside the plates, and held her chair, then led her out of the restaurant.

Now, it was dark everywhere except for a sliver of something vaguely pale just behind the farthest westerly rims, and even then if one looked directly at the paleness, it vanished. The trick was to always look either just above it or just below it.

They turned, heading northward towards the Carbeau place, walking slowly because this was the last sweet moment when they would be together.

Josephine said, 'Sometimes I feel a thousand years old.'

He grinned, unwilling to let their magic moment disintegrate. 'Sometimes you act it.'

'Walter King!'

He laughed, then said, 'Well; sometimes you look so utterly fatalistic.'

'Without reason, Walter?'

'I didn't say that, love. Of course with reason. Only it always reminds me of a — madonna — when you sit very still and seem so far away from me.'

'That's the squaw in me,' she said, and smiled.

'No. That is the *woman* in you, love. I never thought much about it until I met you, but women seem somehow to have some special, deep knowledge about — well — a lot of things. And they seem sometimes to be fitting everything that happens into some kind of context, so they'll be able to guess what happens next.'

He blinked at her. Then he laughed again. 'Lord, one winter in old Jacques's cabin and I emerge in the summertime a full-fledged philosopher.'

'It won't hurt you. Anyway, you are right. What I keep trying to make sense out of is — is why? Why do I love you and why do you love me, and why are we like this when nothing can really come of it? Why can't I just kiss you and watch you walk down the road? That's how it's going to end for us, Walter.'

He suddenly took her by the shoulders and turned her roughly to face him. They were far enough along towards the Carbeau cabin now that no one else was around, which was perhaps a fortunate thing because his action now was not gentle.

'It's not going to end for us like that at all! I give you my word about that.'

'And your brother . . . ?'

'Listen to me Josephine, I'm not saying I have the answer. What I'm saying is that it's simply not going to end for us. Nor like that.'

She raised a cool palm to his face. 'All right. I never wanted anyone to be right so much in my life. Now come along.' She turned, felt for his hand and resumed her way with him at her side. 'Walter, when people aren't bothered very much with ethics and appearances . . .'

'Not that way either,' he said a trifle harshly. 'That's the *easy* way. I'm not looking for any easy way for us.'

She snuggled close and paced along with her head down, pleased and poignant at the same time. Maybe there really *was* a way; certainly he was very strong and resourceful. But *she* couldn't see it.

Maybe, though, women, who were so wise in the ways he'd mentioned, were not supposed to also be wise in the ways that were peculiar to men. She thought this must be so. She also speculated that if the *male* mate was supposed to understand how to fight his way out of this kind of a dilemma, then surely *her* mate would do it, because he was highly intelligent.

They halted outside the Carbeau cabin. Lights were glowing from the windows and a hint of smoke-fragrance came down to them from the kitchen stove-pipe. She read the signs and said she would bet him a kiss that her father and Jacques McLaughlin were sitting in the kitchen with rum-laced coffee, fighting to the death in a no-holds-barred game of draughts.

She would have won the wager, but that wouldn't have prevented her from yielding up the tribute; she did it out there in the soft-warm night before they even went near the cabin door to ascertain what her father and old Jacques were up to.

19

An Approaching Crisis

The last thing Josephine did before kissing Walter at the doorway was to remind him of the letter Pete Sancroix had mentioned being at the store, so the next morning Walter dropped round.

Sarah was tending the counters. Pete, she said, was out back opening crates to replenish the shelves. She got the letter, then had to go to wait on a bitterly complaining holidayer who was lamenting the fact that she had tender pink flesh, and all the previous night out at their camp beside a creek, despite the tent her husband had erected as protection, hordes of the most unreasonable mosquitoes chewed on her.

Sarah watched Walter read the letter,

then turn as though to depart, but those two men who worked for his grandfather appeared in the doorway. They nodded and Walter nodded back. He was pocketing the letter, but Sarah saw the blue eyes and the tawny-tan eyes flick downward at that gesture, then up again to Walter's face.

By the time Sarah got the fat woman taken care of Walter and the large men were over by the large old cast-iron stove. There hadn't been a fire in it for several weeks now, but the battered old captains' chairs were still carelessly grouped in front of it, and that made the area exclusive and inviting. The three men sat down over there.

Sarah did not hide from herself the powerful curiosity she would never have admitted to others, as the three men made desultory conversation.

Caroline Laughlin came in, saw the men seated by the stove, and whispered to Sarah that probably, whatever was to happen was being settled over there right this minute.

Sarah merely shrugged and went to get the five-pound bag of sugar Caroline wanted.

A little later, after Caroline had departed and the two large men rose to also leave the store, Walter sat on as though in deep thought. Sarah went over, finally, to tell him there was hot tea in the storeroom, where her husband was working, but he only thanked her and did not take her up on the offer, and somewhat later when Walter had also walked out, Sarah went to the storeroom to let Pete know all that had happened.

He listened, bending over an opened cardboard carton, then shrugged. There was just so much anyone could do, he told her, and beyond that it was all up to Walter.

He did not speculate on what had been in the letter, nor upon what Walter and those two large men had discussed, which was a disappointment to his wife. She went back in to the store just as Josephine Carbeau entered from the sunlit roadway.

Sarah said, 'Walter was in here a few minutes ago, talking to those two men his grandfather sent.'

Josie smiled softly. 'I know. I was with Walter a few minutes ago.'

Sarah's lagging interest firmed up immediately. 'Trouble?' she asked, and Josephine's fading smile strengthened.

'Always trouble,' she replied. 'Sometimes more trouble than other times. Walter was going back with them the day after tomorrow. But now he's changed his mind. He got a letter from his brother.'

'Something from his brother couldn't be bad news too, could it?'

Josephine didn't get an opportunity to answer. Jacques walked in, casting his thin shadow all the way to the counter. He nodded without speaking, ran a dark gaze over the tobacco counter, pointed to the particular box of cigars he fancied, and put down a small coin for one smoke. Afterwards, as he slowly peeled the foil from the cigar he said, 'Josie, when does the other one arrive?'

Sarah pricked up her ears for Josephine's answer. The girl said, 'Tomorrow. Have you talked to Walter too?'

Jacques clamped down on his cigar and fished for a light as he nodded. 'Just now, up the road.' He flared a match, puffed heartily, savoured the taste and aroma of the cigar, then removed it and critically peered at it. 'All winter I have maybe six, eight of these things, but around here I smoke one or two every day. It probably isn't good for me.' Jacques's black eyes twinkled ironically. 'Well, what they say on television about tobacco killing a man . . . I'm past sixty, so how long would I live anyway?'

The women smiled and Jacques plugged his stogie back between his teeth, was briefly silent while he puffed, and eventually dropped his eyes to Josephine once more.

'If the other one comes tomorrow, it

may change things.'

Josephine didn't appear convinced of that. 'Perhaps, but I can't imagine how. I think they will return together.'

'And take those other two with them?'

Josephine shrugged. 'That won't matter. If Walter returns with his brother, there won't be any reason for those other men to stay in McLean.'

Jacques continued to enjoy his cigar, but this appeared only a physical occupation, his thoughts seemed turned upon something else. 'Well,' he said, just as several customers turned in at the doorway, which put an obligation upon Sarah to depart, but she didn't, she waited for what Jacques had to say. 'Well, tell me one thing, Josephine. Is he going back?'

The beautiful girl nodded without speaking.

Jacques looked steadily at her. 'Your father says if he does that, after fighting against doing it for so long, he will probably never come back to you. Is that so?'

Now, the customers were looking a little impatiently over at Sarah. She ignored them, waiting for Josephine's answer. It came softly.

'I don't know. I wish I *did* know. He told me he *would* come back, and I want to believe that. But I am afraid that his grandfather is very powerful.' Josephine forced a crooked smile. 'Maybe, if he leaves with his brother instead of those other two — then just maybe — he will return to me.'

Sarah finally had to hasten away. At the counter old Jacques fell to studying his cigar again, impassively and silently. Josie reached to lay fingers lightly upon his arm, then step past and go towards the door. As she turned right, up the yonder sidewalk, old Jacques leaned upon the counter and thoughtfully sent up little fat puffs of cigar smoke.

Walter was out in the garden-patch with her father when Josephine got back home, and none of them were aware that the reason she'd gone down to the store in the first place had been to buy sugar and paraffin and pectin, to use in putting up blueberry preserves.

Walter and John had been talking as they re-set the bean-poles in warm sunlight, but when Josephine came around the side of the house, saw them, and started on over, they checked whatever they'd been saying and greeted her with smiles, and silence.

She planted herself firmly before Walter. 'Everyone wants to know if you are leaving at the end of the week. Sarah didn't ask, she wouldn't do that, but when Jacques and I were talking about it, she hung on every word. And what did you tell Jacques about the letter from your brother?'

'Only that he's coming up here. Why look so upset, Josie?'

She started to make an exasperated retort, saw the steady way her father was gazing at her, paused to seek better words, then she said, 'Because, my love, aside from *me* not wanting you to go — for reasons we both understand — I'm beginning to get a bad feeling about Jacques and the others.'

John moved closer. 'Bad feeling?'

Josephine nodded at her father. 'Jacques looked pretty grim when I said I thought Walt would be leaving. For heaven's sake, whatever happens we don't want all these other people to get into trouble about it, do we?'

Both John and Walter stared. The younger, taller man frowned a little as he spoke. 'How — get into trouble?'

'I don't know,' burst out Josephine. 'But if I were to guess I'd say old Jacques might step in and try to prevent you from leaving McLean. And Walter, he's one of the older people; they haven't always admired the legal and ethical procedures.'

John sighed, fished out a handkerchief and mopped his damp forehead. It was hot out there in the garden-patch.

Walter looked sombre as he considered what Josephine had said. Finally he sighed, shoved his hands into trouser pockets and gave his head a little annoyed shake. 'I'll go and find Jacques and tell him everything is all right.'

'Is it?' asked Josephine.

He shook his head at her. 'Of course not, but like you said, we don't want everyone getting involved.'

Josephine's father said, 'Wait. Let me talk to Jacques.' John put up his handkerchief and looked around for the old battered hat he'd left propped upon a bean pole. 'It will be better if I go, than if either of you go.'

There was probably a good deal of truth in this, so neither Josephine nor Walter interfered when John grabbed at his hat and went stamping out of the soft earth to the solid area beyond, and continued hiking away from them as he dumped the old shapeless hat upon the back of his head.

Josephine twisted to watch her father leave, then turned back. 'What did your grandfather's men say — or did you tell them Sanford was coming?'

'I told them. They didn't act very pleased, but they were polite about it. Of course they ran right down to the boarding-house to telephone New York and let my grandfather know Sandy was due here tomorrow.'

'And?'

He flopped his arms at her. 'How would I know, love? Maybe Sandy told Grandfather in advance. Maybe he is even coming because of some new proposal the old man has in mind, I don't know. I told you what the letter said — only that he would be arriving by hired car tomorrow and wanted me to be sure and meet him at Sancroix's store. That it was urgent and very important.' He moved out of the garden to Josephine's side. 'That kind of writing means *something*. Sandy doesn't use words like 'urgent' and 'important' unless he means them.'

He took her arm, turned and started towards the rear of the cabin where a

262

great square slab of shade was.

She walked limply, as though she were very tired. 'I never wanted to just give up before,' she murmured to him. 'I always felt that your grandfather's real strategy was to wear you down — or wear me down.'

'It was,' he conceded. 'That's how people wage their wars in his league. They keep the other person off-balance, and while they're doing that, they also try for the little advantages. It works.'

'Not with us, though.'

'No. Not until now at any rate.' He stopped her near her father's old rickety backyard chair along the rear of the house where the shade was deepest and pushed her down. 'But after what you just said, lover, I'm beginning to get a kind of sick feeling that it *might* work with us.'

She forced a weak smile. 'A mood, just a mood. People get them. Women, especially, get them. And it *has* been a long struggle, hasn't it?'

He nodded, leaning with both hands

upon the arms of her chair. 'I've made a decision, though. To hell with the inheritance, Josie.'

She was shocked. 'You don't mean that, Walter. There's never been anything else but that one objective.'

'Yes there has. You. At first I thought we could breeze through a fight with the old man, and mark-time until the end of this month as well. But he knew better, and now I also know better. I've dragged you through an awful lot of unnecessary hell, just for an inheritance I don't really care about — I only made a point of it because I knew if I got it my grandfather would curl up with anger. But that's over. Tomorrow, regardless of what Sandy says, we are going to go down to Quebec and get married. He'll be our witness.'

She leaned back in the chair not speaking, not able to speak because she was unable to think of the right words. Of course she wanted to marry him; had wanted that for as far back as she could remember, right at this moment, but it seemed as futile for him to give up his goal now, as it must have seemed to him a moment before when she'd mentioned being on the edge of giving up.

Certain that statement of hers had triggered his abrupt response, she now shook her head at him. 'We'll do neither, lover. I won't give up, and you won't throw everything over this close to the end of the month.' She pushed his arms away, rose and said, 'Come along with me to the kitchen, it's almost lunch time.'

He trailed after her obediently, and that meant, at least for now, he as well as she, had a stiffened resolve.

20

War-Council

News of fresh developments brought together those whose lively interest in the King-Carbeau matter made them emotional as well as physical allies of Josephine and her young man.

They met right after closing time down at Sancroix's store. It was close to dinner time so Sarah suggested they have a spot of tea, which was done, and although Jacques, John Carbeau, Pete and Sarah were there, it was not a planned meeting at all. They had just happened to be close by and had dropped in, all excepting John, and he had been at the store to pick up a bag of tinned goods, which were still on the counter when Sarah made the offer of tea, and afterwards, when

John eventually departed, he forgot his purchases.

Jacques was of the opinion that Sanford King just might be coming to join forces with the two men old Everett King already had at McLean. His suggestion, dour to the point of grimness, was that someone ought to intercept Walter King's brother before he reached the village and turn him back.

'That'll only make things worse,' argued Sarah. 'But if this other King does spend a lot of time with his grandfather's men, possibly one of us could keep an eye on him and make sure, then warn Walter.'

Pete Sancroix, who had been most involved at the outset of all this, said glumly he thought none of them could do anything, really, that regardless of their best intentions it was all in Walter King's hands. 'If he doesn't want to go back, he doesn't have to and he knows it.'

'But he's going back,' said John.

Jacques crossed to the stove and sat in one of the old chairs over there. The others were still at the counter near the cash-drawer; in fact Pete and his wife were behind that counter, leaning upon it. Jacques flapped his arms at them, 'I spent the winter with Walter. He didn't say much about his private affairs. But he *did* mention his old grandfather a few times. Now I think that if he goes back, that old man will keep him from ever returning.' Jacques shifted his black gaze to John. 'That's not a fair thing to have happen to Josephine.'

John, usually a quiet, mild man, had no comment to offer, although he most certainly was as acutely aware as any of the others of his daughter's dilemma. Sarah prodded him a little.

'John, what Jacques says is the truth. It's not fair to Josie.'

Carbeau turned his mild glance to Sarah. 'You're right. But what your husband says is just as true: It all lies in the young man's hands. Even if we ran his grandfather's two men out of the village and even turned back his brother, Walter is still the one who has to make the final decision.'

'No,' said Sarah. 'It's that old man down in New York who is forcing him.'

John smiled. 'An old man in New York can't force a grown man who happens to be his grandson to do anything, Sarah. If Walter can be forced . . . ' Carbeau shrugged and fell silent.

That seemed to sum things up rather well as far as John was concerned, and Pete Sancroix, leaning upon his counter looking as solemn as an owl, probably shared Carbeau's sentiments, because after John had spoken, Pete very gently inclined his head.

Sarah was not yet willing to be passive. 'I think if someone could reach that old man,' she murmured, and because this was even more far-fetched, the men gazed at her until, uneasy under that stare, she said. 'We can't just stand here and watch an old man ruin Josephine's chance for happiness.'

'That's already settled,' said her husband. 'One way or another.' He roused himself slightly to add: 'But I don't think Walter will give up that easily. Eh, Jacques? You spent the winter with him; you know him best.'

McLaughlin considered his answer carefully. 'Like I've already said, he didn't talk about his personal affairs. But as a man, I would say he is very stubborn.'

'You see,' crowed Pete Sancroix.

'Being stubborn may not be enough,' went on old Jacques, looking straight at Sancroix. 'That old man down there in New York is very rich and very powerful. Maybe he can't stop his grandson from being in love with John's daughter, but from what I understand, that's not the question anyway. He just doesn't want Walter to marry yet. Who knows what an old man like that will think of?'

'The whole thing,' stated Pete, 'is whether Walter loves Josephine enough to defy the old man.'

'No,' growled Jacques. 'Pete, he's been defying the old man for a long time. Probably they didn't get along before Walter ever met Josephine Carbeau. So it's a personal fight between them. The old man may use Josephine some way to get at Walter. He may have a number of other tricks up his sleeve. But Josephine seems to me to be only caught in the middle.'

Sarah, a little confused by McLaughlin's words and logic, reverted to her central theme. 'They are in love, Jacques. And they love each other. They have no friends but us.'

Jacques flapped his arms again. 'All right, Sarah, what can we do? You don't think we ought to turn back the brother, and maybe running those other two men out of the village wouldn't help either. What, then?'

Sarah pointed to the wall-telephone. 'Call that old man right now. Try to reason with him.'

For a moment everyone looked at

the telephone. Then they gazed at one another. Finally, Jacques shook his head. 'He wouldn't listen to people he doesn't even know.'

'How can you be sure of that?' shot back Sarah. 'All right; if you don't want to do it I'll make the call myself.'

Pete drew up a little from his leaning position and craned around for a look at his wife. Finally, he shrugged. To Jacques and John Carbeau he said, with more than just a trace of resignation in his voice, 'What can happen? It will cost me maybe five dollars, and that old man will hang up in her ear.'

Sarah took this to mean tacit agreement and marched over to the telephone. All she knew was Everett King's name, and the city where he had his offices, but as it turned out that was enough, for although no one was at the office this time of evening, Sarah was able to get the old man's residence telephone number and have her call put through to that address.

Pete, John and Jacques were as

motionless as carved idols while they listened to all that transpired. Sarah turned, while she waited for the call to be completed, and explained what was happening. They had already guessed so they nodded and waited.

Finally, a man's clipped, very professional-sounding voice came down the line to Sarah asking who she was and what she wanted.

Sarah faltered at the outset, at last aware of the enormity of her interference. But she braved up, gave her name, where she was calling from, and said she wished to speak to Mr Everett King.

The male secretary's brisk reply was: 'I imagine so, madam, and so would a lot of other people. But I'm afraid it's impossible.'

Sarah persisted. 'It's about his grandson, Walter.'

That time the man's voice crackled loudly enough for Pete and John and Jacques to hear it distinctly. 'Walter? Has anything happened to him?'

Sarah seemed to believe she could channel this sudden fear into a direct conversation because she said, 'If you'll put Mr King on the line I'll explain to him.'

But the secretary reverted at once to his earlier chilliness. 'Impossible, madam. But if it will help any, my name is Charles Gordon and I am Mr King's confidential secretary. Anything you would like relayed to him can be said to me.'

It was obvious Sarah was not going to get through but she made one last effort. 'Mr Gordon, if you will tell me that when Sanford King arrives in McLean tomorrow he won't be his brother's enemy, there won't be any trouble here. But if he's coming to help those other two men his grandfather has up here, then you'd better tell your boss that Walter has a lot of friends up here who aren't just going to stand by and see him bullied.'

The male voice did not change tone and the clipped words sounded exactly as they had before, when Charles Gordon replied. 'Madam, I didn't know Sanford King was going up there, which means that neither did my employer. As far as I know, Mr Sanford King is at his residence right this minute. If he's actually going to McLean, you can be assured he's not doing so because his grandfather sent him. In fact, madam, I'm sure that had his grandfather known of any such intention he'd have stopped it at once.'

Sarah was holding the telephone-receiver away from her ear so the others could hear. The male secretary paused once, then resumed speaking.

'As for Walter having friends up there, madam, and your intimation that they will protect him, that's all very noble, but I think you have Mr Everett King confused with some gangster. I can promise you there will be no overt trouble.'

Sarah had her answer about Walter's brother's visit, at least about one part of it — Sanford wasn't coming because his grandfather had sent him — but the real purpose of her long-distance telephone call was not going to come to anything.

She rang off, walked back behind the counter over beside her husband, and while the men watched, she raised her dark glance and said, 'Something was wrong.'

Pete rolled his eyes ceilingward. 'What? The man said Walter's brother wasn't being sent, and he wouldn't let you talk to the old man down there. Well, people like us can't just pick up a telephone and call someone like that. There is nothing wrong. Well, there is nothing wrong that hasn't been wrong right from the start. But at least it's looking better.' Pete turned to Jacques and John Carbeau for substantiation. 'Eh?'

They didn't reply. Sarah was the only one of them who had heard *all* that conversation. Obviously, both the other men were thinking of that. Jacques finally said, 'What was wrong,

Sarah? What did he say to make you think that?'

'Nothing exactly. It was more of a *feeling* I had.'

Her husband snorted. 'You see? Look; there is nothing we should do now anyway. First, we've got to wait until this other one, the man named Sanford, arrives. After that, who knows?'

John nodded, glanced at the wall-clock, saw that it was almost nine o'clock, which seemed to surprise him, and said he thought he had better get along home.

Jacques rose to go along with Carbeau, and after Pete had let them both out of the front door he turned to beckon to his wife.

She came, slowly and thoughtfully as though seeking to define or analyse her own feelings. After she had reached the sidewalk Pete double-locked the front door, dropped the key into a pocket and went trudging along beside her in the direction of home. After they had covered about half the distance he looked sideways at Sarah.

'The trouble with women,' he said, 'is that they aren't rational. That man on the telephone said just one thing that makes all the difference. That Walter's brother is coming here without the old man's knowledge. Now then — the brother certainly can't be on the old man's side if he's doing that, can he?'

Sarah turned, studied her husband's testy expression briefly, then retired behind every woman's best defence, she smiled gently and nodded her head. 'You are right,' she murmured, and moved a little closer to her man.

Pete's annoyance, if that was what it was, seemed to dissolve a little at a time as they walked through the very pleasant, warm and starlit night. As they turned to go through the little sagging gate of their house, he was even gallant enough to open the gate and stand aside for her to enter first, something a married man who had shared his connubial estate with the same woman as long as Pete had, only did when he had something stirring in the back of his mind.

Sarah stepped through, turned and waited for Pete to close the gate, then, still wearing that small, knowing, gentle little smile she paced along beside him up to the porch. When he bent to unlock the front door she said, 'How does warmed-over roast beef sound, for supper?'

Giving the door a grand push and permitting his wife to enter first again, Pete said it sounded delightful. He also said, 'And that bottle of burgundy I have in the closet. How does *that* sound?'

Sarah's dark eyes glistened. She didn't answer. She just smiled at him.

21

Alone Together

There was a little breeze the next morning early, and if the wind blew differently any time of year around the Portage Valley countryside, it was because it was never hot.

Even in mid-summer when one of those infrequent little zephyrs arrived, it always seemed to have been cooled by some snow-cap or highland meadow snow-bank before it reached the warmer, lower regions.

In July and August, the hottest periods of the year in Portage Valley, in the whole of Quebec Province for that matter, when a stray little breeze blew, it was chilly.

Josephine explained that to Walter as they picked their way along a trail leading northwest from the village.

Of course the fact that it was early morning, only half an hour or so past breakfast, made the faint bite of that ruffling little breeze more noticeable. She also said those early-morning little winds never seemed to linger much longer than ten o'clock.

He had her father's packboard on his back with their fishing gear and picnic lunch. It was neither a very bulky nor heavy load, and as he followed her he scarcely heeded the little wind. After all, as he said, he'd wintered out at the McLaughlin cabin on its rocky promontory, and when those blizzard-winds had come making it impossible to see ten feet ahead, he got to understand what wind really was.

She looked at the sun a time or two. They were supposed to be back in the village in time to meet Sanford. They had no actual knowledge of when he would arrive, but assuming he'd spent the night down at Quebec, he probably wouldn't arrive in McLean before noon.

This was her idea. They both needed to get away for a while, even for a few hours, and her father had told her at breakfast which creek and which eddy would be best for their purpose this morning.

But he had also told her that with all the holidayers there were about this time of year, it was very possible they wouldn't find any fish left anywhere close to the village.

She felt that was probably true, but after they paused on a rib of gravelly sand and could see one of those camps down nearer a creek, she said there must be some fish left. It was after eight o'clock and everyone down there was still in bed excepting one tousle-headed young boy who was lying in the shade of a fir tree reading a picture magazine.

Where the trail broadened, they walked side-by-side. Where it narrowed he dropped back and let her lead. About a half mile before they came to the dog-leg where their particular creek swung back upon itself, then straightened up and went on again, the trail didn't widen so much as the scrub-brush fell back leaving only bunchgrass and a few frowsy old bull-pines to impede progress so they walked along together once again.

She stopped back about a hundred feet, twisted one way, then another way, and finally pointed eastward. 'We'd better cast from down there. Our shadows will be behind us.'

He shed the packboard, got out their fishing equipment and began assembling it. He was grinning. She bent down to make certain, then she said, 'What's funny?'

His eyes danced when he answered. 'You, and that stuff about the shadows having to be behind us.'

She said, 'City man!' with scorn, then fell to her knees in front and watched him put the lures on their fishing lines. 'I love you, city-man.'

They laughed. Then he started to drop the pole he'd been assembling, though she rocked far back beyond his reach and sat there smiling. 'The best time to catch fish is before the sun rises. Second best time is just after it rises but before it turns hot. So maybe you'd better hurry up with the equipment.'

He smiled. 'You distract me. Why did you have to wear a blue sweater? And when the sun strikes your hair . . . .' He rolled his eyes and made an exaggerated groan. She blushed, jumped up and went closer to the creek-bank, following it westerly until she was well above the eddying dog-leg. There, she turned and made a sober, long study of the water.

He finished with the poles, the lures and reels, and stood up watching her. She was just as alluring that far off as she was up close. He told himself that although he had spent quite a bit of time in Europe, in Florida, California, even New York and New England, he had never seen a woman who had the beauty, the suppleness, the colouring, or the character she had. In fact if someone had told him it was possible to get so much of each in one woman, he wouldn't have believed it.

He hoisted the poles, leaving the packboard and their tablecloth-wrapped picnic lunch behind, and went down to where she waited, dark gaze softly on him until he stopped and said, 'Whatever was I thinking of? I don't want that damned inheritance, Josie. I want you.'

She held forth one hand. 'My fishing pole please, city-man.' When he handed it over she smiled up at him. 'You must be terribly clever, because you are going to have both.'

'What I was thinking about was the kind of a fool I've been to make you go through all this just — .'

'Walter,' she interrupted firmly. 'Evenings are made for talk. Right now do you see how fast that sun is rising?' She started walking eastward, but back from the edge of the creek. He followed after her, trudging along as though the fibre-glass rod weighed a ton. He wasn't really very interested in fishing at any time; right now, this quiet, fragrant, beautiful morning alone out in the valley with Josephine Carbeau, fishing seemed somehow almost sacrilegious.

She showed him where to stand when casting, and true enough, their shadows were behind them. Her first cast was graceful, the line settling back, then spinning forward with the grace of a wind-tossed cobweb. Where the dry-fly landed the water was scarcely disturbed at all.

He went through the same motions. The cast was good, but the drift was wrong; he'd struck water too far out for the tide-drift to carry his lure closer to the shadowy bank where the fish would be lying, deep. They wouldn't rise for a fly where the sunlight was, she told him, so he reeled in and cast a second time. It was better.

She was concentrating on her line and lure. He was concentrating on her. She blended perfectly with this wild and primitive environment. He had taken her to some of the most exclusive restaurants and clubs down in Quebec, and she had blended just as perfectly down there.

Finally he said, 'I don't care if we get back in time to meet Sandy or not.'

She shot him a look, then returned her attention to the dry-fly. It bobbed slightly. She had her mouth open to speak but suddenly she froze. The second time the lure bobbed it went completely under. That time her line sang taut and the dry-fly was gone. She hauled, reeled, and gave slack, keeping up the proper tension, not allowing the trout to get sufficient slack to expel the hook, nor yet keep enough strain on the line to tear the hook loose.

Obviously, she had done this many times before. Walter forgot his own line and lure as he watched her battle the fish towards her, bringing it carefully down-stream out of the eddy and into sunlight where she could see it.

In fact he was watching so intently

that the first tug on his own line went unnoticed, but the second one, a hard strike as though the trout had hit his lure from one side, captured his attention at once.

Josie saw that other strike. 'Get him out of the deep water,' she called, and moments later she said, 'Walter, don't let him have so much slack!'

He picked up the slack but not with the same degree of concentration she was using. 'You sound just like a nagging wife,' he said. He'd never before said anything like that to her; she turned swiftly and looked at him — and that was as long as it took for her hooked trout to get his three inches of slack and fling off the hook, drop like a plummet and disappear back into the shaded, dark water.

She watched her limp line settle upon the water. When her dry-fly surfaced it was soggy, bedraggled and useless. She said, 'Damn!'

He had never heard her swear before and blinked, but surprise did not divert him as it had her. He continued to play his fish until it was near the grassy bank, then he said, 'Don't just stand there pouting — beach him!'

She went ahead, knelt low, caught the fish, not the nylon line, and lifted him from the water to the grass by the gills. He was large and beautifully speckled, sleek and shiny.

She said, 'Three pounds at least. He's beautiful.'

Walter dropped the pole, went ahead, removed the hook and held the fish to the sunlight where it glistened like flashing metal, writhing in his hand. Then he bent and let it slide over his palm back into the water. It spanked the water just once with its flukes and curved downward with the speed of light.

Josephine sat back on her haunches looking from where the fish had disappeared, up to Walter. 'It was a splendid one,' she said, almost wistfully. 'Larger than the one I had.'

He sank down at her side and

proceeded to scrub his hands clean in the salt-grass. 'City-man,' he said. 'I don't have the instinct for it.'

'If you were hungry?'

'That would be different. Of course I'd have kept him.' He raised crinkled eyes as though uncertain whether she either understood or approved. 'I'm going to be a terrible disappointment to you in things like this, Josie. I haven't had a decent killer-instinct since I was twenty years old and used to go up to Vermont for the goose hunting.'

She laughed at him, then threw her arms around his neck and kissed him hard before he could raise his hands. Then she broke free and said, 'Did I really sound like a nagging wife?'

He was still aroused by the kiss. It took a moment or two to come back down from that, so his answer was tardy. 'I was kidding you. But you did sound like one, I guess. I can't recall right off-hand ever having heard too many of them though.'

'Sanford's wife?'

'Oh no; you'll like her. If they ever argued I never heard about it.'

'Is he that compatible?'

He studied her expression for a moment, then shot a look at the sun. 'I'm not forgetting, if that's what you're hinting at. Come along, let's eat. Since we can't fish and you run every time I grab for you, we might as well eat.'

It was actually only slightly more than two hours after breakfast, but on the other hand they had been hiking briskly along for most of that time, so they didn't have to force their appetites.

Walter took their food over under one of the shaggy old pines. The little wind had ceased some time earlier. It was very still now, and warm, and pleasantly fragrant in the shade where Josephine spread the tablecloth and put out their food. There was a chilled drink she had made of blueberries, and that amused him. He said that if there were no blueberries the entire area around Portage Valley would probably never have been settled.

She smiled right along with him, but she also told him that he was accidentally correct; that the oldtime Indians counted blueberries in season as their most dependable crop, and they fire-dried the berries too, then pounded them into the fire-dehydrated strips of meat which were called pemmican, and that was what they lived on through the worst winters.

He was curious about pemmican. She made a face at him. 'When I was a little girl there were still a few old people who made it. Awful; my father would nudge me when someone offered me a bite, and I'd smile, but it tasted like the sole off an old boot — a dirty old boot at that — and the longer you chewed it the bigger it got. Lover, I'm sure glad you palefaces came along so we could have fillets and roast beef and rack of lamb.'

It was very pleasant there beneath

their old pine tree. After he had eaten and was replete he lay back with his legs pushed out to their full length, and crossed both hands over his stomach. Without a hint of a smile he said, 'Squaw, kiss me!'

She bent dutifully, but first caught both his hands to control them, and kissed him. As she drew back just an inch she said, 'Not squaw, beautiful paleface — *klootch*.'

He frowned. 'What? *Klootch*? It sounds terrible.'

'Doesn't it though. Anyway, that's what squaws were called.' Her dark eyes teased him. 'It sounds almost as hilarious as — spouse.'

He lunged but she still controlled his hands, so he fell back, pretending exhaustion, and the moment her hold loosened he got free and caught her by the waist.

She didn't struggle, but laid her face upon his chest, heard the strong, hard pulse of his heart, and sighed very softly. 'I'd die if anything happened to you, Walter. Or to us.'

'Nothing will happen. Sandy will be best man. Tomorrow we'll go down to Quebec and — .'

'No, we won't! Not until the end of the month.'

'You sound like you want that inheritance pretty badly, love.'

She sat up so swiftly it caught him unprepared. 'I don't want that inheritance,' she exclaimed, black eyes smouldering. 'Only you. If I never saw a dime of that old man's money I'd be very happy!'

'Then we'll go down to — .'

'No! You made an issue of it with that old man. You are not going to give in now. At the end of the month we'll be married.'

He smiled. 'Okay; put your head back down and stop looking like an indignant wife.'

She returned to her former position, only this time she reached as far around him as she could get with both hands.

They lay like that until he almost

dozed off, then they sat up again and said they were sad about having to go back to that other world, but began to gather up their gear for the trek back.

22

Death Comes!

They did not permit the unpleasantness lying ahead to make the trek back to the Carbeau cabin gloomy, although inevitably it had a sobering effect upon them both.

Shortly before reaching the outskirts of the village Walter paused to glance back out over the valley. There were many miles of brush, grape, willow-bush, berry thickets and the taller, tougher, more thorny varieties of growth that seemed only to grow where pines and firs, and an occasional blue spruce, did not grow. Above it all was an umblemished sky marked by drifting little irregular ranks of puffy white clouds.

Westerly, he saw the jutting little flaky promontories thrusting forth into the valley from the forest. Beyond sight, off in that direction, was where he'd spent a winter learning some fascinating things he would never use again: how to make mink and otter scent, how to snare wolves who were following the trapline to eat the trapped animals, how to read the winter stars, and tell by scent when, and from which direction, the blizzard was coming.

He turned back, saw Josie smiling, and smiled back. 'You are a mind-reader,' he said, stepping ahead and catching her hand as they moved into the village.

'Was it an interesting winter?' she asked.

'Like visiting another world, Josie. Like stepping back in time to a day when the only really serious thing people thought about, was staying healthy; everything else pretty well took care of itself.'

They saw the sleek but soiled car parked in front of the Carbeau house, and involuntarily gripped fingers a little tighter.

He no longer dragged his feet. 'Let's get it over with,' he said, and hastened forward.

When they reached the house no one was inside so they went out to the back, but no one was back there either. He wrinkled his nose, 'Wherever they've got to, Jacques is along. I know the smell of those cigars.'

She stood in front of the house gazing down the main thoroughfare. 'Maybe they took him to the store.'

'Why there?'

'It's the community centre,' she said, and looked at him. 'They aren't feeling very friendly towards him, perhaps we ought to hasten along.'

He said no more as they left the yard, but he propped John's packboard and their fishing equipment against the front of the house before walking away with her.

It was beginning to feel noticeably warm, finally. There was a sort of hazy quietude about the village as though the heat had reached people, which it had, and already there were grumbles about too much summer, too much heat and dust, and too many strangers although as a matter of fact the entire area probably didn't get more than three or four hundred holidayers all summer long.

They passed two raven-haired youths trying to coax an old car into running. One started to swear when his companion saw Josephine Carbeau coming, and nudged his friend. The angry youth stood with pent up, smouldering fury until Josie and Walter had gone past, then he called the old car some choice names. But it still refused to run.

As they were passing a little café two men emerged almost in front of them. One limped, less than before but still limped, while the other one, big and blue-eyed and thoughtful-looking, gazed at the walking couple and gravely inclined his head.

'Be leaving today,' he said to Walter. 'It's been a tough assignment.'

Walter, with Sancroix's store in sight, merely nodded and kept walking. The two large men stood watching, then slowly turned and started off in their own direction.

At the store two pretty girls were being waited on by Sarah, otherwise the big room was empty. She looked up, seemed surprised when Josephine and Walter entered, then excused herself, came round from behind the counter and approached them.

'They are in the back room,' she said, jerking her head to indicate a storeroom — the one where she made tea and which doubled, occasionally, as Pete's office.

Walter frowned. 'Why there? Is my brother here too?'

Sarah nodded. 'Go on in,' she said, pointing, and smiled.

Sarah Sancroix did not give her smiles freely. Josephine, with a sudden, inexplicable lift of spirit, laid a hand upon Walter's arm as though gently to guide him. He didn't need that slight encouragement though, and started past Sarah at once.

The storeroom door, visible where two counters were kept apart by the little pathway to that room, yielded easily under Walter's hand. He stepped through with Josephine on his heels.

It was cool in there, and gloomy because of only one side-wall window which was both high and narrow. The room had a pleasant odour of coffee, onions, spices and other food.

Jacques was sitting on a bag of dried beans with a tin cup of tea in one hand. He was relaxed and almost amiable-looking. John Carbeau and Pete Sancroix were on chairs which had evidently been brought to this room for this special occasion, and all around them were laden shelves and neatly stacked bags of flour, sugar, potatoes, beans, the bulk-sale items that were usually sold out of bins in the front of the store.

There was a tall, thick-chested man perched upon the edge of a large wooden crate who was dressed in an open-throated plaid shirt, a light gaberdine jacket and cotton trousers. His clothes were too new, his face too pale, his bearing too different for him to ever have been mistaken for a native.

When he saw Walter he slowly smiled and got up off his improvised chair to shift the tin cup of tea to his free hand and extend the other one.

'Hullo, Walt,' he said, sounding pleased. Then the bright, clear blue eyes moved to Josephine and lingered there alive with interest and masculine appreciation. 'You'll be Josephine,' he said, freeing his hand and nodding gallantly. 'I'm Sanford King, Walter's brother.'

The others were still and silent, watching all this.

Josephine smiled at Sanford King. That odd little feeling she'd had in the other room was heightened by the stranger's strong smile, by his ease of manner and his total lack of stress. She moved away from Walter to go over beside her father.

Walter wasted no time. 'I'm not going back with you,' he told the smiling, slightly older man.

Sanford King nodded as though he had expected nothing different. 'No need to,' he said, and fished for a paper that was stuffed into a jacket pocket. He handed it to Walter, but the younger man made no attempt to look down.

'What do you mean — no need to? Grandfather sent you, didn't he?'

'Walt, Grandfather didn't know I was coming up here.'

'Then why are you here, Sandy?'

'Well, Grandfather came to see me a week or so ago, Walt, and he told me what his newest plan was. Either you returned and knuckled under, or he would use me to get to you.'

'And you got mad, Sandy?'

Sanford King seemed about to answer that question. He kept gazing at his brother, then he slowly shook his head. 'It doesn't matter what I told him. You see, Walt, he died in his sleep the very next night.'

It was like having the roof fall upon them; something no one would ever for a moment have thought possible.

Evidently the others, excepting Josephine of course, already knew this because except for shooting looks at Walter, who was standing there stunned and stiff, they continued to sit relaxed with their cups of tea.

'Grandfather — died . . . ?' Walter muttered.

His brother looked a little sardonic. 'You know, on the drive up here I've been trying very hard to find a tear. He wasn't really all bad. After all he did take over the business and build it into something . . . '

'Died, Sandy . . . ?'

The elder King stopped speaking and nodded his head. He allowed Walter to recover slowly before speaking again. 'No one lives forever, you know, Walt, and he was very old. He admitted to being seventy, but he actually was past eighty. I know, because I had to dig up the statistics for the news media. Even so, we had to keep the knowledge out of the newspapers for eight hours so that we could apprise the syndicate's executives first.' Sandy put aside his half-empty tea cup. 'The doctors said it was all very natural; that he had the heart of a horse, but even that kind of a muscle tires and wears out eventually.'

Walter looked for a place to sit down, found a bag of potatoes handy and slumped there. 'Then it's all over,' he said, 'unless you have some intention of taking up where he . . .'

Sanford's eyes sparked softly. 'What are you talking about? You're still in shock or you wouldn't even think such a thing. Look; you can stay up here all the rest of your life, if that's what you want. As for the syndicate — you are equal owner with me. That's how the old man's will reads. I suppose he could have changed it, but he'd also have had to change the corporate by-laws, and I'm not so sure he'd have been able to do that, since you and I, as next in line majority shareholders, outnumbered him. Anyway, Walt, you can come back, open your own office and help me freshen up the place, or you can retire up here. It's strictly up to you. And there's one other thing — that inheritance you're to receive at the end of this month — in another couple of weeks — you can have that today. I talked to the attorneys about it.'

Josephine was pale when her father turned, looked up, then reached for her hand nearest him and patted it without speaking a word.

Walter finally turned. His eyes met Josephine's dark glance. She smiled and he smiled back.

Old Jacques searched his pockets and found no cigar, which wasn't surprising since he never bought but one at a time, and Pete Sancroix scratched his curly black head with pleasurable vigour. He finally pointed to a partially opened door in the rear wall. 'Goes to the alleyway,' he said. 'If you two would like to leave now without having my wife nail you with a million questions.' He looked at John Carbeau. 'Sarah and I will bring the food tonight, John, and she will cook it, and we can have a proper celebration. All right?'

Carbeau smiled his mildest smile and gave his daughter a little nudge, heading her towards Walt King as he nodded. 'I'll go home and get things ready. Come with me, Jacques.'

For Walter and Josephine the rest of that afternoon was like a dream. They did, in fact, leave the storeroom of Sancroix's store by the back door, and once outside where the shadows of buildings mitigated the heat, they started northward hand-in-hand without any real destination in mind until he mentioned going back out where they had spent the morning.

They could never make it and get back in time for dinner, she remonstrated, but she knew a place, much closer, and just as private — out there where Caroline Laughlin had taken her to pick berries that time Caroline, in league with old Jacques, had managed to get them together.

That is where they went, with the sun beginning to slide off-centre a little, in the flawless heavens, and with the sounds of the village behind them, growing smaller and less audible as she briskly walked over the gravelly path leading the way.

He finally stopped, just short of Caroline's private berry patch, and said, 'I didn't believe it.'

She turned and smiled. 'I wouldn't have wished it to happen.'

He swept her into his arms and kissed her so hard her lips were bruised and she gasped for breath. Then he put her down, threw back his head and let off a great roar. She shook her head, tugged at his hand and started onward around that little flinty knoll to the spot where she'd been standing when she had looked up and had seen him standing over there in the tree-shade, smiling.

It was only about half past two in the afternoon. They wouldn't be expected back at the cabin for dinner until an hour or so before sunset, which gave them about four hours to be alone out there. It had been a long and arduous struggle, but now they had won, and four hours wasn't really long enough for them to celebrate, but it would be enough for them to complete all those plans that had meant so much to them both, but which had been left dangling for so long.

THE END

Other titles in the
Linford Romance Library

SAVAGE PARADISE
Sheila Belshaw

For four years, Diana Hamilton had dreamed of returning to Luangwa Valley in Zambia. Now she was back — and, after a close encounter with a rhino — was receiving a lecture from a tall, khaki-clad man on the dangers of going into the bush alone!

PAST BETRAYALS
Giulia Gray

As soon as Jon realized that Julia had fallen in love with him, he broke off their relationship and returned to work in the Middle East. When Jon's best friend, Danny, proposed a marriage of friendship, Julia accepted. Then Jon returned and Julia discovered her love for him remained unchanged.

PRETTY MAIDS ALL IN A ROW
Rose Meadows

The six beautiful daughters of George III of England dreamt of handsome princes coming to claim them, but the King always found some excuse to reject proposals of marriage. This is the story of what befell the Princesses as they began to seek lovers at their father's court, leaving behind rumours of secret marriages and illegitimate children.

THE GOLDEN GIRL
Paula Lindsay

Sarah had everything — wealth, social background, great beauty and magnetic charm. Her heart was ruled by love and compassion for the less fortunate in life. Yet, when one man's happiness was at stake, she failed him — and herself.

A DREAM OF HER OWN
Barbara Best

A stranger gently kisses Sarah Danbury at her Betrothal Ball. Little does she realise that she is to meet this mysterious man again in very different circumstances.

HOSTAGE OF LOVE
Nara Lake

From the moment pretty Emma Tregear, the only child of a Van Diemen's Land magnate, met Philip Despard, she was desperately in love. Unfortunately, handsome Philip was a convict on parole.

THE ROAD TO BENDOUR
Joyce Eaglestone

Mary Mackenzie had lived a sheltered life on the family farm in Scotland. When she took a job in the city she was soon in a romantic maze from which only she could find the way out.

NEW BEGINNINGS
Ann Jennings

On the plane to his new job in a hospital in Turkey, Felix asked Harriet to put their engagement on hold, as Philippe Krir, the Director of Bodrum hospital, refused to hire 'attached' people. But, without an engagement ring, what possible excuse did Harriet have for holding Philippe at bay?

THE CAPTAIN'S LADY
Rachelle Edwards

1820: When Lianne Vernon becomes governess at Elswick Manor, she finds her young pupil is given to strange imaginings and that her employer, Captain Gideon Lang, is the most enigmatic man she has ever encountered. Soon Lianne begins to fear for her pupil's safety.

THE VAUGHAN PRIDE
Margaret Miles

As the new owner of Southwood Manor, Laura Vaughan discovers that she's even more poverty stricken than before. She also finds that her neighbour, the handsome Marius Kerr, is a little too close for comfort.

HONEY-POT
Mira Stables

Lovely, well-born, well-dowered, Russet Ingram drew all men to her. Yet here she was, a prisoner of the one man immune to her graces — accused of frivolously tampering with his young ward's romance!

DREAM OF LOVE
Helen McCabe

When there is a break-in at the art gallery she runs, Jade can't believe that Corin Bossinney is a trickster, or that she'd fallen for the oldest trick in the book . . .

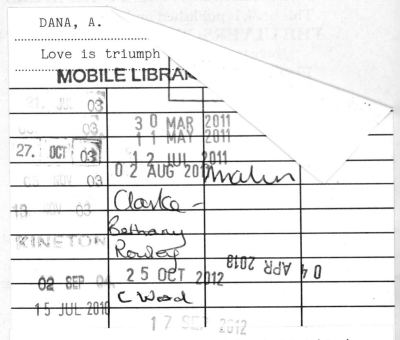